To my father
for having transmitted

his love of classical mythology to me

A fictionalized history of the Trojan War

This novel is based freely on Homer's Iliad

ENGLISH VERSION TRANSLATED BY
ROSEMARY DAWN ALLISON

PREFACE

I n a book published two years ago, entitled *Triangoli diabolici*

indagine su un archetipo del male (Diabolic triangles Investigation of an archetype of evil) , among others, is written:

"Jealousy is *an omnipresent sentiment. Moreover, it is one of the main declinations of the human soul, which has been found since the dawn of time and is substantially detached from historical and social conditions. It is of no coincidence that classical mythology represented and typed it*"[1].
And the concept is better defined further on:
"*In the myth* ...., jealousy *is the midwife of tragedy and of blood*".[2]

Here we take this feeling for granted, always susceptible to alarming deviations, it represents the other face of love: both one and the other state of the soul, preeminently they move human actions and, within the myth, even the Gods themselves.

The war of Troy, with its enormous burden of pain and death, begins right from a love triangle whose sides are: Helen, "femme fatale" *ante litteram* of the Homeric legend; Paris, hero with a classic virile charm; Menelaus, pale ruler of Sparta, overwhelmed by the continuous confrontation with his valiant brother Agamemnon.

---

[1] Musci, A. - Minicangeli, M. 2006. *Triangoli diabolici. From Rina Fort to Circe della Versilia. Investigation of an archetype of evil,* Rome, Alternative Press.
[2] Ibidem

The meeting between these characters activates a destiny that is filled with *pathos*: Paris, son of King Priam is madly in love with Helen, and runs away with her; Menelaus, Helen's former husband, blinded by jealousy and lust for revenge, declares war on Troy, beginning a ruinous tragedy that will last ten years.

Around this central nucleus, infinite events are linked to each other by the invisible Fate who comes to life, now tangling now dissolving: unfathomable and mysterious, a true *deus ex machina* of Greek mythology, Fate exceeds, with its absolute determinism, even the will of the gods.

Like the Iliad, to which Cristian's writing refers, as with all the myths of antiquity, far from simply proposing an invented story, he has fulfilled the same function that today is assumed by psychoanalysis. Dense with symbolism, in fact, the myth dug deep into the human soul triggering them to become aware of their hidden drives and freeing them from the slavery of the unknown.

The love triangle therefore comprises the underlying dynamic – he-she-the other – on which infinite variations are implanted, according to a space-time scenario that never repeats itself in its fundamental instances. And this happens as much in real life as in artistic re-enactments, especially in theater, cinema and literature.
The story of Helen, Paris and Menelaus therefore represents "an archetype", a primary model that recurs in the complex logic of human feelings. To the point of being considered the archetype of absolute evil.
It is not strange then if the Homeric plot, despite the passage of entire centuries, each time returns to enthrall and involve.

A few weeks ago, all of a sudden, this very fluid and captivating piece by Cristian urged me to turn my mind to the lost pleasure of "listening to stories", that ancestral childish disposition of following mythical stories, from the fantastic narration of grandparents, to the compelling plots of fairy tales and legends.

I began to read and continued until the end, without taking a breath, often pausing on the pages because, continuously, names and situations were linked to innumerable details that had been long submerged in my crowded memory. The tightened synapses regained their height leading me to readings that seemed to have been forgotten.

So I returned joyfully to my years in high school, when, among students, they joked mocking the intricate and improbable events of this noisy acolyte, made up of characters and divinities who, between malice and passions, often touched the fascination of madness.

Yet, imprisoned in spite of ourselves between books and old benches, we would never have admitted then that, after all, those events had won us over. It might happen that, at the end of the lesson, an intense curiosity remained to know the implications of that story that we dealt with solely as a scholastic duty.

Those who claim the Homeric poem is nothing more than the harmonious and poetic result of a tradition handed down orally are right: the conflicts and situations reported in it adhere too closely to earthly existence.

With this fictionalized version of the Trojan epic, it seems that Cristian proposes winking, between the inviting and the amused. A sort of game ... almost a bet.

He seems to already know that the readers will remain, despite themselves, caught up in the plot and that, like children placed before a fairy tale, at the end of each chapter they will ask with irrepressible curiosity:
"And then?"

Consiglia Mosca

Mottola, 10 June 2009

CONTENTS

PROLOGUE

In the time when humans, gods and heroes were the only

true masters of their time, intertwining their lives, confusing their work, assimilating and sharing their feelings, fate revived, as it had already done millions of other times, as it does every day despite our being unaware and as it will do until the final day of human existence, the historical, fantastic and mostly intimate story that has marked and conditioned the natural course of history with it extraordinary action, dynamic narrative, epic plot, psychological implications, and eternal indelible values.

PROMETHEUS, THE WEDDING OF THESIS AND PELEUS AND THE APPLE OF DISCORD

It all began on a brisk spring morning...

The sun of day, long awaited by mortals and immortals, rose on the mountains of Thessaly.

Finally the divine wings of Hermes, god of luck and travel and messenger of the gods, rested exhausted on a comfortable seat of ebonite, after having delivered the happy invitation throughout creation. Meanwhile, little Eros, god of love, took advantage by playing with the caduceus, in the heartbreaking expectation of hitting the two young spouses who everyone was now awaiting. The world celebrated the wedding feast of Thetis and Peleus.

Thetis, or Tethys, was the most beautiful of the fifty nymphs who were daughters of Nereus, the old god of the marine abysses. Her youth and her bewitching ways had also caused the father of the gods, god of heaven and earth, to lose his head, Zeus, who, despite already being married to his sister Hera, goddess of abundance, used to loose himself in faithless escapades with the most beautiful maidens in the world.

It happened that, just when Zeus, in disguise, was about to mate with Thetis, Hermes arrived in time, bringing an urgent missive to his father: the Titan Prometheus, who had been chained by Zeus for years on a cliff in the Caucasus for having stolen the divine fire and given it to humans, had to report something that if ignored would cause the supreme god to lose the throne and his primacy on Olympus.

Thus, the divine seducer swooped down like a thunderbolt on Prometheus and promised to end his captivity and the atrocious torture to which he had been condemned if the latter immediately revealed what was threatening his throne and had troubled his sleep continuously. And while he was making a solemn oath, he liberated a huge, majestic, impressive eagle in flight, which came with its claws against the vulture that had meanwhile come from the east. Throughout the day that dismal bird devoured the liver of poor Prometheus, abandoning its victim in the hours of night, during which the abdominal organ, by divine will, fatally and cruelly recomposed itself, ready to be devoured the next day. That was the infinite punishment that had been decided by the father of the gods.

Only after the raptor's beak fell to the ground and the eagle returned to its lord's feet did Prometheus raise his exhausted head and, while a light drizzle wet his dry lips, did he accept the compromise dictated by his executioner, revealing that if Zeus conceived a son with Thetis, he would do to his father what his father had done to his grandfather.

At this admonition, the father of the gods was stunned, the sky thundered, a thunderbolt ripped the earth open and the overflowing waters of the Pontus reminded Zeus of the heinous means by which, in the mists of time, he had killed his father Cronus removing him from the throne of thrones.

Prometheus was immediately freed and Zeus renounced Thetis forever ruling that no being of a divine nature could ever join with the daughter of Nereus, who would marry a humble mortal, the strongest of princes then living, Peleus, son of Aeacus, king of Thessaly, the one who after a thousand vicissitudes had managed to seize the golden fleece during a feat while following

Jason and the other 54 Argonauts, that had been brought together
by the centaur Chiron, the one who, although mortal, would have
fought as a god, the one who was most devoted to Zeus and would
watch over his future wife day and night at the cost of his own life.

This is why, despite the heterogeneous nature of the
spouses, the wedding being prepared was blessed by humans as
well as by the gods, that is why the wedding witnesses were Hera
and Zeus in person and that is why gods and goddesses from all
around the Earth, sea and sky flocked to Mount Peleus to celebrate
the sensational event.

Finally, escorted by Apollo's golden chariot, the two
spouses arrived and among a thousand celebrations they took their
place at the center of the table set with the most exquisite delicacies
on the Earth; immediately at their side sat the divine witnesses and
then Poseidon, god of the sea, Hades, god of the underworld, his
wife Persephone, goddess of spring and summer luxuriance;
Apollo, god of the sun and the arts; Ares, god of war; Athena,
goddess of wisdom and fortitude; Aphrodite, goddess of beauty;
Artemis, goddess of hunting; Hermes; Demeter, goddess of the
crops and fertility of the earth; Hephaestus, god of fire and
industriousness; Themes, goddess of justice; Irene, goddess of
peace; Aeolus, god of the winds; Dionysus, god of wine and
games, and so on, up to all the rulers and notables of the Earth.

Everything had been taken care of down to the smallest
detail, everything was perfect, indeed divine, happiness was clearly
visible in the eyes of all the guests and love in that of the spouses,
even before Eros had stretched his bow and let fly his fatal arrows
towards them.

A scent of nectar and ambrosia inebriated and spread in the
air each time the two cupbearers, Ganymede, son of King Tros, and
Hebe, goddess of youth, served all the guests in turn.

Apollo, urged by his father, called upon the Muses (Clio, Euterpe, Thalia, Melpomene, Terpsichore, Erato, Polyhymnia, Calliope and Urania), as well as the Graces (Aglaea, Euphrosyne and the other Thalia) and began to sing the deeds of Peleus, accompanied by the zither.

The sound of that divine instrument enchanted all present and resounded all around the Earth until Iris the deaf and ugly goddess of discord heard about it, the only goddess who had not been invited to the banquet. The previous day, she had attempted to break into the divine gathering but was escorted by Eros and Dionysus who unknown to Poseidon were hidden with the Nereids and the Oceanids.

Even Ares, who after having argued animatedly with Irene had withdrawn with Aphrodite, noticed that suspicious shadow and, grasping her by the throat, made the unwanted goddess tumble all the way down the western side of Mount Pelion, telling her not to return.

But the singing of Apollo and the festive shouting of the participants increased Iris's anger and indignation to such an extent that the latter devised a diabolical plan that would have the most unexpected and unpredictable consequences...

Discord went to the ends of the Earth, where Atlas, brother of Prometheus, had been relegated to support the heavenly vault having been guilty of having participated in the war of the Giants against Zeus. In the garden of the Hesperides, the daughters of Atlas, where the trees with golden apples grew; employing trickery Iris gathered the most beautiful apple and immediately returned to Thessaly with it.

She arrived at the banquet when the celebrations were drawing to a close and the guests, one by one, were showing off the gifts brought for the spouses: Poseidon gave Peleus two beautiful horses, Balius and Xanthus, the fastest in the world, gifted with speech and prophesy, Hera gave Thetis a magnificent peplum decorated with embroidery, Aphrodite offered a bronze cup and a golden diadem, Athena a golden flute, Hermes a bronze and ivory chariot, Chiron a heavy spear with a bronze point.

So, while everyone admired the features of those wonderful gifts, Iris managed to introduce herself into the party and hide in a dark corner where no one could see her but close enough to be able to throw the "apple of discord" on the table, now almost cleared, that she had stolen from the daughters of Atlas.

Although he was not very lucid because of the 99 ounces of wine he had drunk in the competition with Dionysus, Zeus was the first to notice the apple; he knew those fruits well and, before all the others inevitably looked at that extraordinary fruit, he ruled: "it is from the garden of the Hesperides!"

Suddenly everyone were enthralled, including the bride and groom, by that apple that caught the eye at the center of the table and someone assumed it was another gift for that unforgettable wedding.

Again it was Zeus who noticed there was an inscription on that fruit, but the wine he had drunk prevented him from distinguishing the letters well and then he sent the apple to Athena, the most learned among the gods, asking her to read the inscription for everyone. Athena did not hesitate and read the curious message: "To the most beautiful", and returned the fruit to her father so that he could decide who it was for.

She was certain her husband would have no doubts, and made no effort to present the reasons of the bride and first goddess in order to grasp that extraordinary gift. Immediately afterwards

Aphrodite intervened, reminding Zeus that it was not by chance that the title of goddess of beauty belonged to her. Finally other goddesses and nymphs came forward, all with reasonable arguments, but in the end the third candidate gathered around Athena who, in addition to possessing a statuesque physicality, also boasted an indisputable inner and intellectual beauty.

Even Zeus expressed his embarrassment with this contest and, when the murmur grew dramatically to the point of dispute, he uttered a powerful cry like a hundred lightning strikes, silencing everyone. Irate and staggering, he took a few steps away from the banquet, leaving the burden of choice to Themis, goddess of justice.

Themis, in turn, after having convinced all those present that everyone had their own good reasons and that nobody there was able to judge objectively because, for one reason or another, they were emotionally involved, acting on the assignment received, she ruled: "The choice touches Paris of Mount Ida, who is the most beautiful among men".

Only then, Zeus, who could not wait to rest to rid himself of his accursed hangover, expressed his paternal approval of the sentence and decreed the matter definitively closed.

So, after several years, when Paris achieved his maximum youthful beauty, the three candidate goddesses, preceded by Hermes, in their turn departed for Mount Ida.

PARIS' JUDGMENT AND RETURN TO TROY

During the journey Aphrodite, unbeknownst to the other goddesses, managed to seduce Hermes and steal the secret of Paris from him, revealed that night to the god by his son Pan: the young shepherd was actually Alexander, prince of Troy, son of Priam and Hecuba. His parents had abandoned him at birth on Mount Ida, as an oracle had prophesied their son would cause the fall of the entire kingdom of Troy. King Priam, unable to be the cause of *his son's* death, had ordered that he be left on that mountain known to all for the harsh winters and the presence of wild beasts.

The little boy, sent to meet his certain death, was nursed and protected by a large bear and then cared for and raised until he was strong and beautiful by a family of shepherds who, following the bear, had discovered the den and fortuitously also the newborn in the basket.

When Hermes and the three goddesses joined Paris, he was in the shade of an oak tree playing his fistula of seven canes, watching over his flock with satisfaction, unaware of the incredible visitation.

Having revealed herself to the young man, Hera began by saying that, being that it was her privilege to dispense wealth and power to mortals, if she received that prize she would make Paris the richest and most powerful of men.

Athena, on the other hand, in exchange for the apple offered intelligence, wisdom and valor in life and war.

Finally Aphrodite appeared, more beautiful than ever; explained to Paris that he already possessed all that her competitors offered him because he was actually already the son of a rich and powerful father and he already had all the promised gifts and his noble origin soon would be revealed to him. Aphrodite, on the other hand, offered him the love of the most beautiful mortal woman that no man's eyes could resist.

Paris half-closed his eyes, in his mind he saw wealth and power, he was fascinated by the highest wisdom, but with the image of Helen, the woman promised by Aphrodite, he could not help but instantly fall in love and all else dissolved like clouds in the sun; he then opened his eyes and, now blinded by love, without hesitation handed the apple into Aphrodite's hands, disregarding the scorn and threats of Hera and Athena who, defeated, withdrew.

Hermes immediately ran to inform Zeus of the choice Paris had made, while Aphrodite promised the young shepherd that he would soon know his noble lineage and love; however, he would have to race to retrieve the robe that wrapped his infant body in the basket and leave for Ilion as quickly as possible, the splendid capital also called Troy; there he would be registered in the games in the kingdom, where a fat bull was the prize, that days before the king's soldiers had confiscated the livestock from the one who believed to be his father.

Paris, bewitched and dreamily obeyed without delay and, with a rough spear, a bow and its characteristic fistula, finally reached Troy, the "city with golden walls". It stood on a pleasant hill between the Hellespont and the Aegean Sea. At the foot of the hill flowed two rivers, the Scamander to the west and the Simoenta to the north.

There, with Aphrodite at his side, he beat all the participants in the tournament, one after the other, under the eyes of the rulers and Prince Hector, the strongest and most valiant Trojan hero.

At the time of the award ceremony, the winner approached the royal stage to receive Priam's investiture and blessing, but, when he was about ten paces from the king's seat, Princess Cassandra let out a shrill cry of distress; Priam and his lady froze, recognizing only in that moment the clothes the young man wore; only then did they realize that the battered shepherd from Mount Ida, armed with humble weapons but capable of beating all the strongest Trojan nobles, could only be their beloved son Alexander, abandoned tearfully twenty years earlier.

There were festivities in Troy for another 7 days and 7 nights and, despite the initial envy and the dull grudge held by his fifty brothers, twelve sisters and young Trojan nobles, Paris soon managed to be valued and loved by everyone, especially by Hector, his older brother. Only Cassandra continued to distrust and curse whenever she had the occasion to meet up with him, inciting his father and his people several times to ban him from the city before the fatal prophecy could be fulfilled: Troy would be destroyed and his family exterminated in the flames. Cassandra, in fact, at a young age, for having refused to return the love of the god Apollo, had been condemned by divine will that no one would ever believe the prophecies her divine lover inspired in her. The unhappy princess was able to predict all the disasters that affecter her people in time but every time no one trusted her or accorded her their trust, in fact everyone avoided her and considered her not quite sane.

THE ABDUCTION OF HELEN

Some time later, Aphrodite, appearing in a dream of the newfound Trojan prince, ordered her protégé: "Take a ship and go towards the south, you will round the island of Tenedos, you will go down along the wooded sides of Lesbos, you will pass between Pseira and Chios and there you will see two white doves meet, and fly away together; follow them and stop your ship only where they land; in that land you will find the woman I promised you and who disturbs your dreams every night".

Paris, after telling Priam of his vision, gathered fifty young people of his age and, despite Cassandra imploring him and admonishing him innumerable times, he managed to sail with the blessing of his father and the approval of Neptune, who calmed the waters, and of Aeolus, who released favorable winds for sailing.

So the Trojan ship left the homeland and traveled for days until it met up with the doves and lapped the kingdom of Sparta on which, after the death of Tyndareus, young Menelaus reigned.

And the Trojan strangers, who had just landed, came across, precisely, the young king at the head of a garrison ready for war; Paris met him and reported the reason for his pilgrimage to the lord of Sparta.

Menelaus welcomed him as was due a foreign prince and according to what was foreseen by the law of Zeus regarding the sacredness of guests; he had the Trojans escorted and placed at court and asked Paris to remain in Sparta at least until he and his army returned from the expedition that he was preparing to lead against Crete; on his return Menelaus would help Paris with all his power to seek what the goddess Aphrodite had promised him.

Paris and Menelaus were immediately in agreement; almost instantaneously a certain complicity was created between the two, corroborated mostly by the fact that the two regal young men were more or less peers and that Menelaus had certainly not had a happy adolescence, having always grown up in the shadow of his older brother Agamemnon, who, on the other hand, had never known friendship.

On the evening of his departure for Crete, during the banquet, the Spartan king called his bride to entrust the young guests to her during his absence. The order created amazement among the servants; the presence of Queen Helen was in fact very unusual, indeed quite exceptional, given Menelaus' justified jealousy in showing his beautiful wife in public.

As soon as Helen, escorted by her handmaids, entered the atrium of the hall, all the bystanders could no longer take their eyes off her beauty, fresh, graceful, harmony in her young face and in her every movement.

Paris, like everyone else, was enchanted, he could no longer turn his eyes away; he seemed to see Aphrodite in flesh and blood, but an instant later, when the queen was at the marble door, at the same time ecstatic and terrified, he could no longer fail to recognize the woman who was the object of his dreams, the one whom the goddess of beauty had promised on Mount Ida. The most beautiful man and woman in the world were there, facing each other, mutely staring at each other, astonished and blushing like children.

Menelaus noticed how distraught his young friend was but there and then did not give it any importance, being now accustomed to the reaction his beautiful bride aroused in all men; on the contrary, he was attentive and recommended that her and her handmaids should attend to the young prince and his companions during the entire time he would be away from home. So, after the last orders were given, Menelaus left with his army.

In those days Helen and Paris, although they tried to avoid each other in every way so as not to betray the trust of the groom and their friend, they could not escape the divine will that day after day was fed more and more by the flame of passion in the glances of the two beautiful young people: revulsion soon became a fatal attraction the Platonic amorous glances became hot nights amid the silks of the royal bridal chamber.

Helen was now finally in love for the first time, overflowing with joy. Only two things sometimes constrained her sparkling happiness: the sight of her little daughter, Hermione, and the thought that all this would end when Menelaus returned; suddenly her face darkened and the sadness often took on a depressive form, as far as to imitate her mother in attempting suicide; but now Paris was following her everywhere and arrived in time to shield her from that extreme gesture. That same evening Paris told her his story and Helen did the same.

She was the second daughter of King Tyndareus of Sparta and the beautiful Queen Leda, who, after having given birth to the princes Clytemnestra and Castor with her royal husband, was seduced by Zeus who had turned into a swan, when Tyndareus was on a trip to Egypt. Helen and Pollux were the fruit of their union. Leda never revealed her secret and threw herself from the walls of the city of Sparta in shame before her husband returned from the Egyptian expedition. Tyndareus, for his part, raised the princes without any distinction, as if they were all his offspring, and told them their mother had died in childbirth. Meanwhile Helen was becoming more and more beautiful, even more so than her mother, and all the rulers of the neighboring regions came to Sparta to ask her father for her hand in marriage. Tyndareus, now old, was clearly in difficulty: he no longer knew how to justify the continued waste of that indomitable daughter without risking compromising the safety of the crown.

One day the king of Athens, Theseus, killer of the Minotaur in the labyrinth of Minos in Knossos and also secret pretender to the princess, managed to kidnap Helen and take her with him to Athens. The two became lovers and the Athenian ruler decided to reveal the truth about his divine origins to Helen and the circumstances of her mother's death.

Shortly thereafter, however, an expedition led by Prince Pollux brought her back to Sparta by force. It was on this occasion that the incomparable horse tamer, Castor, tragically fell in battle and Pollux asked the gods to follow his brother even in death.

Tyndareus, having regained his daughter but always in need of making allies, identified in the princes Agamemnon and Menelaus the possible saviors of his kingdom; he helped the two to drive the usurper Thyestes, their uncle, from Mycenae and to regain the throne of their father Atreus; so Clytemnestra went to marry Agamemnon and on the occasion of the wedding, on the advice of the wise king Ulysses of Ithaca, he invited all the kings and princes to court who were the pretenders to Helen's hand, he made them swear solemnly: divine fate would decide who would have his other daughter, Helen, and all the others would bless and protect that union in every way and by all means, even declaring war on anyone who attempted to separate what Fate would unite that day. The princes swore without hesitation, and soon Fate decided on the spouse and the successor of Tyndareus on the throne of Sparta: the incredulous young Menelaus.

As Helen told her story, her voice became more and more mixed with hiccups; tears gradually marked her white face with its divine features. Paris wiped her eyes and pushed the blond hair behind her ears, then asked her to stop her painful narrative; he gathered his men around him and ordered them to prepare to leave; he decided that the next day, when the city was still asleep, they would leave Hellas and return to Troy; Helen and her maids who, in the meantime, had met the beautiful young Trojans, would also leave with them.

All evening they celebrated and toasted in honor of Paris. Helen embraced her lover and her head rested on his chest. It was soon time to leave; leaving little Hermione with the housekeeper who had raised her, they ran to the beach hidden under the veil of Aphrodite. There the Trojan ship was ready to take them to the kingdom of Priam.

Aphrodite had kept her promise and her son Eros had never been as prodigal in shooting arrows as with the crew of that ship. However, old Poseidon had no liking for the slight the two lovers were about to make against Menelaus: he infuriated the Aegean enough to make the return of the faithless to Troy nothing short of miraculous.

The love that fears nothing, consciously led those beautiful young people against everything and everyone but, at the same time, gave them that human and at the same time superhuman strength to face any trial, any court, divine and mortal; it even led them to declare themselves guilty in the presence of the Council of Elders of Ilium and to declare their willingness to renounce their rank and go live on their own in a hut on Mount Ida.

After listening to the story of the two tender lovers for hours, Priam, who presided over the Council, looked deeply into the eyes of Paris his son and recognized in that abyss the ardor he himself had felt in his youth and still felt for Queen Hecuba; then he looked at Helen, beautiful among the beautiful, asked her if she really loved his son; he did not even wait for an answer (it was enough for him to look at her for another instant) and, having gathered the strength in his tired body, he stood up and recited his most beautiful and profound harangue in defense of the two young lovers. The Council could not make a reply. From that moment Helen of Sparta became Helen of Troy.

Paris and his beloved, holding each other's hands, ran flourishing with happiness on the streets of the city, exuding and spreading love towards all the motionless subjects staring at them.

THE PRINCIPLE OF WAR

Meanwhile, on the other side of the Aegean, Menelaus had returned to Sparta and, learning of Helen and Paris' escape, invoked the help of Zeus, guardian of the violated sacred laws of hospitality, he quickly recomposed the royal garrison and raced to Mycenae to inform his brother of what had happened.

Agamemnon, while still listening to the fitting resentment, an almost mocking smile became impressed on his rough face, without any compassion or consideration for the suffering of his betrayed brother; on the contrary, he was almost happy about what had happened to his blood relative: the offence caused was the right pretext for to putting to use the plan that had been maturing in his diabolical mind for years.

In the past, in fact, when Agamemnon was still wandering because of his uncle's coup, the fortuneteller Calchas had prophesied that one day he would reign over the entire Aegean. Since then he lived and worked only for that insatiable thirst for power, plotting and insinuating discord within and outside of Hellas. Troy controlled the traffic between the Aegean and the Pontus, between Hellas and Asia and represented the point of reference for all the peoples that still did not already circulate around Mycenae. Now the Mycenaean king had legitimate justification, served on a silver platter; he could not miss such a wonderful opportunity to carry out his project.

Agamemnon, however, also knew that in order to wage war on Troy he needed to assemble the largest army ever on the field and that a very large fleet was needed to take it to the other side of the sea; this would require skillful diplomacy and most of all a lot of time. First of all, he sent Menelaus to Troy to officially request the return of Helen from Priam and the payment of a large amount of bronze and gold to compensate for the serious offense suffered. He then asked the wise and cunning Ulysses, king of Ithaca, to accompany his inexperienced brother on the mission and sent messengers and ambassadors with rich gifts to all the kingdoms of Hellas in order to ask for military help for the expedition, reminding the Achaean princes of the sacred oath made in the house of Tyndareus. In a few years he transformed all the seaside towns into industrious shipyards; the forests were stormed for the wood required to build the ships, for which thousands of Phoenician workers and engineers were called, masters in naval art.

In Troy, despite Ulysses shrewd rhetoric, Menelaus' bitter rancor and violent threats against Priam caused the enterprise of the two Achaeans to fail, as Agamemnon had foreseen.

Meanwhile, the first armies were ready and, slowly confirmation of participation in the war began to arrive in Mycenae from all parts of Hellas, ships and men began to gather in Aulis.

In Search of Ulysses and Achilles

However, only two noblemen of importance were lacking, indeed their contribution was fundamental to the successful outcome of the expedition: Ulysses of Ithaca and Achilles of Phthia.

The first, son of Laertes, also called Odysseus, after having quarreled with Menelaus precisely in front of Priam and therefore was guilty of having quenched the only hope of avoiding the imminent conflict, on his return from Troy he too had started to prepare ships and armies alike, but, after marrying the beautiful and wise Penelope and having a son with her, he made believe he was insane in mind whenever there was a messenger from Agamemnon he refused them his help.

Thus, the king of Mycenae, aware that in battle, apart from strength of arms and valor, wisdom and cunning are required, decided to entrust the final attempt of persuasion to Palamedes of Nauplia, wise and shrewd prince, who went in person to stony Ithaca to ascertain Ulysses' alleged madness for himself.

Arriving in Ithaca, Palamedes found king Ulysses by the sea, awkward and unsure on his feet, with a spear and a plow; he tried to plow the sand and ordered his servants to spread salt as seeds, in order to generate vast plantations. Palamedes watched him for a long time and for a while, he followed all that Ulysses did and said, he seemed to believe he was mad; however, he decided to stay a few more days in Ithaca imploring the god Hermes to provide him with a solution that could unmask what so many of Mycenae believed to be a pretentious simulation by the Ithacan king.

Every day Ulysses could always be found on the beach and while he was plowing he was thinking about how to send his guest away as he was making him increasingly uncomfortable; that bizarre situation was beginning to be unsustainable.

He was about to leave, when Palamedes, looking at the wet nurse who carried Telemachus, Ulysses' newborn son, had a brilliant idea: he asked the wet nurse to take the child to his father in the hope that this vision could revive him. However, when he was on the beach, the ambassador of Agamemnon placed Telemachus on the ground a few meters in front of the oxen and incited the animals to pull the plow. At that point Ulysses straightened up, immediately assuming his typical prowess, in the aspect that all Greece knew and with a shout he leapt in front of the oxen, picked up his son and hugged him to his chest with rough tenderness, fulminating the shrewd Palamedes with his eyes. It was the proof that the latter had been looking for.

The astute provocateur then smiled and said: "Oh Ulysses, son of Laertes, king of Ithaca, even you pretend! You have never been mad. There is no one wiser than the one who renounces war to enjoy his bride and family. However you swore an oath in the presence of your fellow men and gods and now is the time to respect it!"

Now unmasked, Ulysses replied: "Well said, astute Palamedes, I respect your intelligence as much as your lineage and I am grateful to you for calling me back to duty, even if I withdraw from the happiness of husband and father. Also tell Agamemnon that I will be with my men in Aulis at the new moon and I will wage war on Troy, but, remember, I will be your friend no more for what you have done today."

And while he caressed his son's head and the sun went down on the sea, the king of Ithaca looked at Palamedes, who satisfied, climbed on the ship that would take the best news back to Agamemnon.

Prince Achilles, however, had completely disappeared. Every attempt by legates and informants had failed, so much so that the princes in Aulis had now decided to do without him. However Agamemnon, who had questioned his fortune teller Calchas on the outcome of the war, knew very well that the answer was clear: "To conquer Troy you must conquer the hero who represents the extreme defense of the city, the great Hector, and only the strongest of the Achaeans can do this, the invincible Achilles, the hero born of Peleus and Thetis."

Then he waited for Ulysses to arrive. The Council of kings convinced the king of Ithaca to go in search of Achilles in Phthia in Thessaly.

There Ulysses learned from the now mature Peleus that his son Achilles had been taken away by his mother Thetis, who, from birth, had tried in every way to have her son made immortal, who at the behest of Zeus had been made mortal; she had almost obsessively subjected her baby to the test of fire after having smeared him three times with ambrosia and had made him invincible by completely immersing him, holding him by the heel, in the waters of the river Styx. However, all the mother's desperate attempts proved to be in vain: when, on Mount Othrys, the god Hermes asked the young Achilles to choose between a long and quiet life with a peaceful death in his home and a short but intense life, full of glory in life and death, the fearless son of Peleus had no doubts, opting for the second.

Ulysses believed the great Peleus and, knowing that he could not obtain any information from his wife Thetis, did not even insist on involving her; instead he decided to go to the city, to fairs and to emporiums, disguised as a merchant, until he managed to obtain a clear idea about where to look for the immensely strong prince: one summer's day he learned that on the island of Skyros, in the reign of king Lycomedes, lived twelve maidens who were the king's daughters, to whom for some time a thirteenth with a mysterious past had been added.

Thus, Ulysses bought the most beautiful fabrics from Sidon, Tire, Crete and Egypt and left for Skyros. Once there he convinced King Lycomedes, by way of his usual enchanting stories, to show the wonderful fabrics to his daughters.

The girls immediately treasured the merchandise and the gentle manner of that strange merchant. At one point, while the princesses chose the most beautiful items handing them from one to another, Ulysses showed them another saddlebag, making believe that it contained the centerpiece of his merchandise. The curious women instinctively threw themselves on the bag and opening it discovered a helmet of admirable workmanship and a clean and shining sword; suddenly surprised they withdrew and looked at the merchant as if to request an explanation. The thirteenth girl, who had been in a corner all the time trying in every way to disguise the features of a muscular physique, unlike the others, showed a certain interest in those beautiful weapons and, coming forward, could not resist the desire to try them. Ulysses, then, blocked the wrist that was already ready to raise the sword in the air and explained that that object was not a woman's jewel but was destined for a young hero who would accompany him to Aulis, where an army awaited him, that would soon leave to conquer Troy; the strongest city in the region would be conquered only if that hero was there to threaten her. At these words, the thirteenth girl put down the helmet and clasped the sword more tightly in the fist saying: "That man that came, the foreigner! How do you know all these things? Where are you from? Who are you? You are not a merchant, are you?" And Ulysses promptly replied: "No, I am not a cloth merchant, as you are neither one of Lycomedes' daughters nor a woman. You are a man, the strongest of men, the invincible invulnerable Ulysses, prince of the Myrmidons. Take off those unworthy vestments, oh hero, and answer the call of Agamemnon who offers you the most beautiful gifts and promises you the most sought-after share of the spoils, as well as the chance to gain glory on the field."

Achilles, who for some time had regretted having put himself in that embarrassing situation to say the least, to obey the maternal will, then came out into the open, returned to Phthia to rally an army and, taking with him the heavy spear that his father had received as a wedding gift from the centaur Chiron, harnessed the two immortal horses Balius and Xanthus, given to his father by the god Poseidon himself, he sailed with his best ship at the time to Aulis, escorted by the charioteer Automedon, by his faithful friend Patroclus, as well as the usual shrewd Ulysses, who, pleased, admired that extensive mobilization of Myrmidons that he had finally managed to bring to Agamemnon.

THE OFFENSE TO ARTEMIS AND THE SACRIFICE OF IPHIGENIA

It was in this way that the 50 ships of Achilles of Phthia joined the 100 under Agamemnon of Mycenae, 90 under Nestor of Pylos, 80 under Idomeneus of Crete, 80 under Diomede of Argos, 60 under Menelaus of Sparta, 60 under Agapenore of Arcadia, to the 40 under Ajax of Locris, to the 12 of Ajax of Salamis, to the 11 of Ulysses of Ithaca, etc. etc., up to counting hundreds and hundreds more under the orders of the kings of Elis, Aetolia, Rhodes and the Aegean islands. Each ship had more than a hundred men on board.

Never before had such a thing been seen. It was the most massive deployment of forces that History could recall... A myriad of well-armed men led by the best known and brave Achaean warriors could have overwhelmed any enemy power. Agamemnon assumed supreme command of the Achaean expedition and all were now ready to sail.

The day before the scheduled departure, while the holds of the ships were being loaded with abundant provisions and weapons, the kings and princes decided to measure themselves in the hunt, since that territory was famous for the extraordinary flora and fauna present.

The king of kings, Agamemnon, to reaffirm his primacy over all (not always unanimously recognized), passed everyone on his splendid stallion; following a woodcock, he set against it with his three dogs. Fast as lightning, on the other side came the mighty Achilles, who, leaped down from his horse, threw out his net to the maximum and captured the magnificent bird under the eyes and nose of the Atreides.

They continued along a small river and shortly after Ajax of Locris signed to Agamemnon the presence of a lively hare that unsuspectingly bathed its muzzle in a puddle on the opposite bank. Agamemnon attempted a circling ploy to capture the beast from behind as the other kings advanced, but the formidable Ulysses, who had no equal with the bow, let fly his fatal arrow even before anyone succeeded in crossing the river and the prey was his.

The king of kings, then, struck his pride twice causing his bravado to seem ridiculous, he furiously gave chase to a young fawn with frightened eyes; almost madly he galloped on his horse, entered the thick wood so that the other leaders could not keep up with him. His steed foaming at the mouth by now but the Atreides was more than ever determined to capture that beautiful and extremely fast deer. At a certain point the animal stumbled into a high bramble permitting Agamemnon to be upon it, he jumped off his horse, grasped the spear with all his might and threw it violently at the defenseless flank of the prey which, with eyes imploring for pity, stared at its eager executioner. The deer called desperately, collapsed, raised itself on two of its legs, fell back. The dogs were on it, however, two arm lengths away from the still trembling body, they stopped suddenly and, out of respect, lowered their ears and tails. Agamemnon was also perplexed and surprised by the behavior of his infallible hunting dogs; looking at his skewered prey, his heart stopped beating momentarily, but immediately after he smiled and, hearing the voices of his rivals nearby, he prepared to take the spear from the animal's body and to load the beautiful prey on his horse to show it off as soon as he could before all the other kings. Proudly the Atreides exclaimed: "Cursed deer, I finally

captured you, you're mine! Everyone must see that not even
Artemis could protect you from the infallible actions of
Agamemnon, son of Atreus!" The Achaean kings finally
congratulated their champion and together they returned to the
camp.

The next day the sacrifice and propitiatory rites were
performed and everyone embarked with great fanfare. The sea,
however, was flat as a table, without even the slightest ripple, and
the wind was calm as never before in that area; no leaf moved, how
could the Achaean sails swell?

It was decided to wait on the ships. Hours passed, the sun
ran its full length and hid behind the mountains of Boeotia, but the
sea and the wind showed no sign of changing. Agamemnon was
then forced to give the order to return to land to spend the night
there.

The same thing happened the following day, as did the
third, fourth... On the tenth day, the Achaean kings, tired and
impatient, closed themselves in council. Nestor was convinced that
behind this extraordinary phenomenon was the discontent of some
divinity, and suggested asking an oracle. The proposal was
accepted and Calchas was called, the diviner of Agamemnon, who
immediately made a statement: he would reveal the cause of the
divine misfortune that affected the Achaeans not before all the
sovereigns and princes present there had committed themselves
with solemn oath to curb their rage and anger at the one who would
be directly involved in the matter. Agamemnon, impatiently, swore
to all, making himself the guarantor that no one would dare to raise
his hand against his protégé and ordered the oracle not to delay any
further and to speak. At that point the bard revealed that some of
the bystanders had acted sacrilegiously towards the goddess
Artemis by breaking into a forest sacred to her, killing a deer that

was dear to her and uttering haughty, offensive words towards Olympus. Following this Artemis had invoked and obtained from Zeus that Aeolus and Neptune would restrain the winds and seas.

Suddenly all eyes were on Agamemnon who, unable to pull back, recognized his responsibility for the offense and then asked Calchas how to expiate the mistake. Apollo's oracle lowered his eyes to the ground and after reminding his master once again of his previous promise, he continued, still uncertain, saying: "Artemis, virgin goddess, requests the sacrifice of a mortal virgin to appease her anger. Not an ordinary virgin but one of the daughters of the one who caused the offence."

All those present trembled with sacred terror watching the face of the Calchas bard change color and hearing the fierce shouts of the supreme chief who swearing devoured the mouth of the poor oracle with his gaze. Agamemnon seemed to have gone mad, with unspeakable rage he immediately chased everyone away and, after having destroyed everything in his tent, he called a handful of his most loyal soldiers to him and ordered them to go to Mycenae and collect little Iphigenia, his adored who he had had with the noble Clytemnestra.

The men, although sad and anguished, obeyed and after many days they returned to Aulis with the young princess.

Everyone was called together. The priests prepared the rite of sacrifice. The oblivious Iphigenia, in front of her petrified father, was immolated on the altar, dressed in a white tunic and crowned with violets and cyclamen. A knife rose on the victim and the sacrifice was consumed as a chill horror ran through the bones of all bystanders.

For a few minutes nothing and nobody dared to break that immense silence, but then, suddenly a sure wind rose from the west rippling the waves and inflating the sails. "To the ships!" – cried Agamemnon. Everyone ran to get the last things and quickly filled the black keels that were now foaming on the sea towards the Troad.

THE LOSS OF PHILOCTETES

The crossing was not brief, notwithstanding when having the winds in their favor; the huge Achaean fleet had to stop several times before arriving on the islet of Tenedos, in front of Troy.

In one of these intermediate stages there were no shortcomings: in a bush of a rich islet, the Thessalian Philocthetes, son of Poeas and companion to Heracles on many adventures, was bitten in the foot by a snake and, although the wound was not fatal it caused the hero great suffering and day by day infected much of the limb; moreover, an unbearable stench emanated from the wound that caused vomiting and discomfort to the rest of the crew, so much so that it was decided, on the advice of Ulysses, to leave the poor sufferer on the island of Lemnos and quickly resume the expedition. Philoctetes tears and prayers begging them not to abandon him to his fate were to no avail. He was only given bow and arrows to arm him, which his dear friend Heracles had dipped in the blood of the Lernaean hydra, which he had given to him on his deathbed.

THE FIRST YEAR OF WAR

Finally the span of ships arrived in front of Troy, quickly filling the entire horizon, now resounded the anguished cry of Princess Cassandra on the mighty citadel.

The Trojan men, led by Hector, armed themselves and lined up on the beach to thwart the landing, while old men, women and children rushed inside the walls. King Priam with the Council of Elders and the priests offered a sacrifice to the gods to pray for their protection. Paris hugged Helen reassuring her that divine will would never permit their love to end.

The following morning, in support of the Trojans, the invincible Cycnus, king of Colonides and son of Poseidon, arrived with his family. As soon as the Achaean soldiers landed on the beach, they launched into the enemy multitude, reaping hundreds of victims. Even Hector certainly did not betray his reputation and managed to face the landing of two ships with a handful of men.

The Achaeans, however, were incalculably superior and they also had the most valiant heroes and princes of Hellas on their side, including the invulnerable Achilles who, wearing the shining armor that his mother Thetis had asked the god Hephaestus himself to make for him, launched furiously on the great Cycnus. The men around withdrew. The combat was horrific; both had divine origins, they could have crushed boulders with their strength, but neither could even scratch the other's body. In the end, however, the Pelides Achilles, instructed by the goddess Athena, abandoned his weapons and pounced on Cycnus to wrestle that monstrosity; the king of the Myrmidons, simulating a hold on his legs, squeezed Cycnus' head in the grip of his left arm and with his right he pulled the heavy, high-necked helmet, until his head was torn off.

At that bloody sight, the Trojans and Hector himself terrified, fled the fight and ran to take refuge within the walls. The Achaeans then gave pursuit, but, despite repeated attacks, all that day they could not breach the citadel. Then came the goddess Selene with her moon to end the hostilities of that first day of war.

The following days the Achaean leaders attempted other massive attacks with different strategies on several flanks but the Trojans promptly rejected any assault. Agamemnon decided to besiege the city to prevent the enemy from finding food and aid from neighboring lands, but Troy remained impregnable and the food seemed to be endless...

Hundreds of men died every day.

Thus the first year of the war passed quickly enough.

CHRYSEIS AND BRISEIS, THE ABANDONMENT OF ACHILLES AND THE REVENGE OF ULYSSES

From time to time the Achaeans raided the lands on the nearby coasts, destroying cities and forests and winning rich spoils for their leaders, especially for Agamemnon and Achilles, who, during the capture of Thebes, at the foot of Mount Placus, killed the king Eetion, father of Andromache (Hector's wife) and enslaved two pretty girls, very skilled in the female arts: Astynome of Chryses called Chryseis, who went as booty to Agamemnon, and Hippodamia of Brise named Briseis, who was taken by Achilles.

Years later, with a rich ransom, old Chryses, priest of Apollo arrived in the Greek camp; he made a protest to the supreme king for the return of his daughter Chryseis. Agamemnon, out of pride, would never have given up the beautiful Thessalian girl; he therefore had the old father cruelly thrown out, ordering him not to appear any more with these claims.

Forcefully dismissed, Chryses weeping, turned to Apollo his protector, and invoked the revenge of the god against the invaders and their commander. The god Apollo could not ignore his priest's tears and, having descended from Olympus with his golden chariot, he began to throw softened lightning bolts on

Achaean animals and soldiers, spreading a deadly pestilence in the field.

The Greek leaders in council questioned the usual oracle Calchas and from him they learned the cause of that death and the only solution that would appease the divine Apollo: was to return Chyrseis to her father.

After long and heated discussion, Agamemnon, cursing his infallible oracle, had to bend again to the divine will and agreed to return his slave; however, in substitution, he asked Achilles for the beautiful Briseis.

The latter, having heard the conditions of the Atreus, instinctively drew his sword and launched himself on that bully, but the goddess Athena herself blocked his arm and made him reflect on the unwise imprudence of raising a hand against the one who exercised supreme power. So Achilles placed the sword entirely up to the hilt and before leaving the Council he decreed: "So be it. You, oh supreme chief, today you will have my Briseis, but you will curse this day and your extreme arrogance. From today you will no longer be able to depend on me and my Myrmidons. You will all regret it!" Saying that, he left the assembly.

Achilles absence was much felt in the days following. In future clashes, the Trojans went from strength to strength; soon the balance began to hang on the side of Priam, who almost every day blessed the arrival of numerous allies, tired of the Achaean harassment in Asia. First of all came Aeneas, son of Aphrodite and Anchises and husband of Creusa, daughter of the Trojan king; then came Pandarus and Sarpedon, son of Zeus, and then Glaucus, prince of the Lyceum and nephew of Bellerophon, with the Meonians, the Pelasgians, the Thracians, the Ciconians, the Paeonians, the Paphlagonians and the Phrygians. Furthermore, discontent in the Greek camp increased and the goddess Iris often sewed discord among the princes. It was also assumed that there was a traitor, since the Trojans and their allies were almost always able to predict Achaean movements.

Ulysses, who until then had been tested greatly for his physical value as much as his expedients and tricks that had been conceived with little difficulty by his very fertile and shrewd mind, took the opportunity of taking his revenge on the one who had stolen him from the love of his son and wife, forcing him to participate in that interminable and senseless war, which claimed hundreds of lives every day: with a diabolical plan he managed to convince Agamemnon and the other kings that the Trojan spy among the Achaean ranks was the rich Palamedes. The latter, was judged publically, and sentenced without appeal; pierced by a rain of arrows, and thrown into the Scamander.

THE DUEL BETWEEN PARIS AND MENELAUS

Meanwhile, Thetis, listening to the prayer of her beloved Achilles, persuaded Zeus, who always had a weakness for her, to punish the king of kings for the offense caused to Pelides.

Thus Morpheus was called, the god of sleep, and sent to Agamemnon to mislead him deceptively that if the Greeks forcefully attacked the following day they would finally be able to conquer Troy.

The supreme commander awoke with a start and awakened everyone even before the sun rose; he ordered everyone to organize themselves and to launch against the golden walls of the city of Priam the most lethal attack that the Achaean forces could unleash.

At the sight of such an imposing deployment, the Trojans also became alarmed, and prepared for the confrontation.

Nine years had passed since the Achaean ships had touched those shores threatening the safety of the great Troy, the most important and richest city in Asia, which had now become a dirty and miserable citadel where people died, now almost oblivious to the glories of the past.

To many it seemed that the fateful day had arrived when the palm of victory would be awarded and the dead counted for the last time.

Hector came out of the city gates with his army.

Enemy hosts advanced proudly facing each other ready to annihilate each other in the name of their homeland.

Menelaus finally saw Paris in the multitude, who, in his shining weapons, clamoring with all the greatest Achaean heroes; immediately the blood boiled in the veins of the betrayed Atreides who, blazing in his face as never before, ran towards him, blinded by the desire for revenge.

Paris withdrew and sent his men forward. His older brother, Hector, witnessing the scene, could not but blame that vile gesture. "Paris" – he said – "you are beautiful as a god but fearful as a girl. You know well the art of seducing women but don't have the courage to face the man whose wife you kidnapped throwing your father, your brothers and sisters and all Asia into the atrocious disasters of an unjust war."

Those words hit young Paris straight in the heart. He repented and, to remedy his action, even before the bulk of the armies came into contact, he proposed a drastic solution to put an end to that infinite massacre: the conflict would end that day with a duel, a duel to the last blood between the proposer and Menelaus; the winner would take Helen, his treasures and commercial control over the entire geographical area.

Everyone liked the proposal, except for the god Ares, who until then had remained impartial to enjoy the spectacle. Priam and Agamemnon took a solemn oath, all consecrated with a lavish sacrifice.

After the necessary preparations, under the eyes of all, even of the beautiful and cursed Helen, the duel began.

Paris first shook his spear, then touched Menelaus, but neither of them hit home. At that point the Atreides took up his sword and dealt a hard blow on the helmet of the young Trojan prince; the headdress withstood the blow and the Achaean sword shattered. Menelaus was then lost, but, taking advantage of the temporary stunning of his opponent, he fell on him trying to strangle him as Achilles had already done with Cycnus, but the goddess Aphrodite was not slow to intervene by loosing the strappings holding the helm of her protégé. Then the Achaean king, having regained his balance, prepared to hit Paris' now unprotected head with what was left of his sword, but immediately the goddess intervened again spreading a thick fog mixed with dust around the two heroes and the arena and finally withdrew Paris from the fury of his rival. When the cloud vanished, only Menelaus appeared, exhausted but alive.

The Greeks shouted victory while the Trojans, stunned, wondered where their cavalier had ended up. The goddess of beauty had already led him to the fortress under her peplum, which made him invisible.

Ares and Athena, however, were unhappy with the solution and the cowardly work of Aphrodite, urged Pandarus to take advantage of the situation of total dismay to shoot his arrow against Menelaus' exhausted body.

This actually violated the pact signed with the Achaeans. Agamemnon, in all his fury, had his wounded brother gathered up, invoked the wrath of the gods and urged his followers to battle.

DIOMEDES AND GLAUCUS

At that point it was no longer only a war between two peoples, between two cultures, but the feeling of pugnacious revenge even fed the souls of the divinities, who like mortals lined up on both sides: Athens and Hera were with the Achaeans while Apollo, Aphrodite and Ares were with the Trojans. Every now and then even Poseidon intervened for the Greeks and Minerva for the Dardanians. All obviously commanded by the supreme Zeus.

The first heroes to meet and take part in epic duels were King Diomedes, flanked by Sthenelus, son of Capaneus, and Aeneas, son-in-law of Priam, who came to Pandarus' rescue.

Diomedes revived in all his epic deeds when he struck Pandarus in the eye with his spear piercing his head and throwing him off the chariot; then he pounced on Aeneas, took a large stone and hurled it against the Dardanian with all his enormous strength, smashing his hip; he could not finish only because the goddess Aphrodite managed to arrive in time to protect her son from the fatal blow.

Meanwhile Ares, alongside Hector, mowed down the ranks of the Achaeans who retreated helplessly.

Hera and Athena judged the behavior of the god of war to be highly unjust and with the consent of Zeus they caused the brave Diomedes, the most fit of the Greeks, to injure Ares in the belly thus forcing him to leave the battlefield.

Strangely, however, at the sight of the arrival of a new hero, Diomedes' terrifying momentum was pacified by the enchantment; as soon as the stranger appeared before him, the brave Greek stopped suddenly as if he recognized a numen in such features, an entity from another world. In reality he was not a god or a superhuman being at all, but Glaucus, prince of Lyceum, son of Hippolochus, son of the great Bellerophon, killer of the Chimera.

Only then did Diomedes understand why he was suddenly so fraught in facing that opponent, despite his fury he had no regard even for the most pugnacious and formidable among the Olympians: his grandfather, Oeneus, years before had hosted Bellerophon in his home for twenty days, in which the two had become good friends and promised eternal peace.

Diomedes and Glaucus climbed down from their respective chariots and shook hands, renewing their ancestors' pact of non-belligerence; after which they exchanged weapons so that in the future they would recognize each other at a distance and would avoid each other; finally they returned to fight in their respective ranks, amidst the incredulity of men and the admiration of the gods.

THE MEETING OF HECTOR AND ANDROMACHE

The fighting between the Greeks and Trojans continued unabated, fierce as ever.

The Greeks, inspired by the great moment of Diomedes and protected by Athena, seemed to have the upper hand, but Hector heroically maintained his position and at times seemed to be able to break through beyond the enemy line; however the Trojan allies suffered the powerful advance of Agamemnon and Diomedes on both fronts.

The most serious problem for the Trojans was that they could no longer count on Ares; indeed, now even Athena was against them. So much so that Hector, on the advice of his brother Helenus, decided to return to the citadel to ask his mother and the other women of his family to go and offer rich gifts to Athena to appease her murderous fury, allowing for a more fair battle.

Before returning to the outside of the Scee gates, where the battle continued to rage, while going to get Paris, Hector became aware of his duty as husband and father, which was imposed momentarily on that of the soldier; he was seized by an irresistible impulse that made him go to Andromache, his bride, and to his small son in swaddling clothes, Astyanax, who knew he could be left an orphan from one day to the next.

Andromache took his hand and in a voice veiled with tears pleaded with him to stay within the walls, to take care of his wife and son before his men, since, if she became a widow, both would meet a certain cruel fate, and become easy prey for one of those ruthless invaders.

The heart of the strongest and most valiant of the Trojans, was dismayed on hearing such heartfelt words, and could not fail to express his displeasure derived from the sharing of the concerns of his relative; nevertheless he definitely could not escape his supreme duty as a Trojan and as a man. Tearing himself away from his beloved wife, he approached the handmaid who held his son; he smiled, took him in his arms and, raising him to heaven, implored the gods: "Let him grow strong and brave, that everyone may admire him and consider him better than his father." Having said this, he kissed him tenderly and placed him in his mother's lap. Finally, looking lovingly into Andromache's eyes, he stroked her face one last tender time and rushed back onto the field alongside Paris who was waiting for him at the gates of the city.

THE DUEL BETWEEN HECTOR AND AJAX TELAMON

The return of the two princes gave new strength to the Trojan army, which quickly recovered the distance lost in the previous hours.

Hector was unrivaled; whoever tried to face him fell beneath his infallible blows. Everyone was terrified of measuring himself against him... but somehow they needed to stop him.

Menelaus, strong for having defeating Paris, blamed his fearful men who were retreating; when he was about to rush himself to challenge the Trojan leader, Agamemnon and the other princes held him back, knowing that he certainly could not stand in comparison to the strongest of enemies.

In place of Menelaus Diomedes, Ajax of Locris, Ajax Telamon, Idomeneus, Meriones, Eurypylus, Thoas and Ulysses were offered, as well as Agamemnon. Fate designated the tall, large Ajax Telamon who, wrapped in shining armor and holding his long and heavy spear, immediately went to meet the Trojan leader.

The two knew each other and held each other in high esteem. They faced each other for a long time without anyone being able to penetrate the armor of the other; it was then decided to move on to the swords, until the heralds of both sides arrived, illuminated and guided by Athena and Apollo; these halted the conflict as night was falling and that day had already been the cause of too many deaths, especially among the Achaeans. Ajax and Hector shook hands sincerely.

Agamemnon looked up at the untouched walls and bitterly remembered the deceitful dream of the previous night.

The following day the Trojans forced many of the Achaean ranks to flee. The Greeks increasingly regretted the absence of Achilles and retreated all together: from being the besiegers and in a few hours they had become the besieged. Even Diomedes, Ulysses and Macau were injured and taken to their tents. Even the ships were now in danger.

The prayers of the old Phoenix and the shrewd Ulysses were to no avail to try to return the invulnerable leader of the Myrmidons to battle. Agamemnon was thus forced to offer the restitution of Briseis and many other gifts so that Achilles would forget the offence he had received, but the latter was adamant, almost heedless of the Achaeans' extremely critical moment.

Only Nestor managed to have any result, breaking through the sensitive heart of the young Patroclus, Achilles' inseparable companion. These asked and obtained the weapons of the Pelides from his commander and friend and the permission to take the Myrmidons back on the field; in this way it would be believed that Achilles had returned to fight, with the double effect of reinvigorating the tired and discouraged Greeks and of terrorizing the ever more relentless Trojans. And so it was.

THE DUEL BETWEEN PATROCLUS AND SERPEDON AND THE DEATH OF PATROCLUS

As soon as he entered the field on the golden chariot

drawn by Balius and Xanthus, the two divine horses belonging to Peleus, it seemed that Patroclus really was Achilles.

A shiver of horror ran over the skin of every Trojan. So the Achaeans, spurred on by their respective leaders, took the advantage to fight back.

The Lycian Serpedon, son of Zeus, who had already shown his worth that day by slaughtering dozens of Achaeans, was the first to react to the counter-offensive: he ordered his parents not to step back as he would face the newfound Achilles himself; thus saying, he gestured to his charioteer Trasimede to proudly direct the chariot towards that of the Pelides.

Patroclus certainly did not retreat and, as soon as Serpedon was within range, he shook the spear, striking at poor Trasimede who died. Serpedon's spear wounded a horse that flanked Balius and Xanthus; the expert Automedon, Patroclus' charioteer, promptly cut the harness with his sword to free the other two sacred beasts.

Taking advantage of Serpedon's temporary unsteadiness, who had taken the place of his fallen charioteer, Patroclus managed to run through his rival, planting the spear between his heart and abdomen; the blow was fatal for the Lycian commander, who at that sight all retreated, taking with them some of the Trojans also.

In a very short time, Priam's coalition lost all the advantage gained on the field in the previous two months. So they returned to fighting under the walls.

In the following hour most of the Trojans had already returned to the city and by now only Hector, with a few other brave men, resisted the deadly Achaean assault.

Agamemnon, was the least satisfied with how amazingly the situation had been reversed, praised the councilors for the strategy implemented and ordered his followers not to advance further, consolidating the positions gained, from which the Greeks would mount the definitive attack the following day.

However, blinded by the success and the desire for glory, Patroclus, ignored the orders of the supreme king, continued to insist on his side; the first clashes proved him right, but then, when he came close to the Scee gates, with a stone he shattered the bone of the good Cebriones, Hector's charioteer, causing his eyes to splash out of their orbits, the god Apollo could no longer intervene; guilty of having dared too much and the sin of pride, the young friend of Achilles was wrapped in a thick fog, his eyes clouded with a dark soot, the ties of his helmet were loosened and his armor was removed, the spear and the shield.

All then saw who was really hidden behind the armor of the Pelides and gradually hearts slowed their beating, as if before a narrow escape.

The closest to Patroclus was Euphorbus, son of Panthous, who, taking advantage of the dismay and nakedness of the young Greek, did not hesitate to place a staff across his shoulders; some of the Myrmidons threw themselves forward to protect their injured leader from further blows, permitting his escape.

But even before Patroclus moved to take refuge behind the ranks of the Achaeans that came to his rescue, the expert Hector predicted and blocked the way out, inflicting the fatal blow to the young opponent: a sturdy spear pierced his belly.

Automedon ran after the sacred horses.

The Greeks were petrified and backed away.

Setting his foot on the corpse and extracting the spear from his body, Hector rose to exemplary punisher of the superb Thessalian and, protected by the divine Apollo, he stripped himself of his weapons to wear the dreaded and much desired weapons of Achilles.

The battle reignited.

Caught in anger and fury, Menelaus managed to get the better of young Euphorbus. Automedon, once he had rescued the horses, he returned to try to recover the corpse of Patroclus and, covered by Ajax Telamon and Ajax d'Oileus, who kept Aeneas and Chromium occupied, he ran through Ares using trickery.

After a furious fight the body of Patroclus was recovered, and the Greeks retreated.

And so, while Hector was taken triumphantly to the city with golden walls, Antilochus had the difficult task of telling Achilles of the loss of his most loved friend.

THE DUEL BETWEEN ACHILLES AND HECTOR

The energetic son of Peleus, as soon as he learned of
the disaster, cast his companions out of his tent with excruciating
screams, threw himself on the ground, tearing his clothes and hair;
at one point he burst into hysterical tears; Antilochus, at a safe
distance, was ready to intervene in the event that despair induced
him to commit suicide.

Achilles' cries and tears were soon heard even by his
mother Thetis, who, appeared in the tent, and in every way tried
comfort him and dissuade him from returning to the field to avenge
his fallen friend, but all her attempts were in vain. She only
managed to wrest the promise from the hero that he would wait
another day to give vent to his terrible revenge, a time in which the
nymph would convince the god Hephaestus to forge new weapons
for her son.

Not a moment longer had passed since the sun gave the first
glimmer of light behind the Troada mountains that Achilles began
to move; Thetis knew this well and arrived with divine armaments
in time. The god of fire, in fact, certainly could not deny any favor
to the Nereid, as she had welcomed and raised him at the time of
his birth, when his mother Hera had thrown him down from
Olympus because he had been born ugly and deformed.

Thus Achilles promptly informed the other commanders of his imminent return to battle; his anger had not been appeased either by men or by gods, but had become atrocious revenge against Hector and the Trojans. His was now a personal war.

The Myrmidons, lightly deployed, advanced furiously before all the other hosts; banging spears on shields marked the march; Mars like Agamemnon enjoyed this.

The Trojans prepared to face that deadly war machine that advanced threateningly before their eyes; fear and despair became irrepressible when they saw the terrible gaze of the fierce Achilles, who stood divine on the chariot, with the new shining bronze, silver and gold weapons at the center of the advancing enemy.

The impact was devastating for the Trojans: they understood immediately that this time Achilles had truly returned; under his blows dozens of enemies fell at a time as if they wielded sickles in a wheat field.

Priam, powerless spectator of that massacre, gave orders to open the doors so that the bulk of his army could return as quickly as possible. Some Trojans fled to the river, but even there, the Pelides' fury pursued them and killed them; in a short while the waters of the Scamander became cloudy and turned red.

Achilles seemed to be an irreducible bloodthirsty monster; in his murderous fury it seemed that he did not want to spare anyone, neither women nor children, he would have killed even the great Aeneas if Poseidon had not promptly taken him away; he was now expected to attack the walls of Troy, where Hector, his bitter enemy, was waiting for him with his own weapons. At that inhuman impetus, even the great Trojan prince was seized with terror: instinct led him to flee together with many fellow citizens who desperately sought shelter within the walls, but the sight of his destroyed homeland, his family and of his slaughtered son, he restrained his heart in his chest, which now, fearless, was intent on facing the mighty spear of Peleus.

The time had finally come: the strongest and most valiant of the Achaeans found themselves face to face with the strongest and most valiant of the Trojans: Greece against Troy, West against East, Athena against Apollo, revenge and lust for glory against defense of values and freedom.

Achilles and Hector scrutinized each other for a few moments while the world moved about with a mad dynamism.

Pelides was the first to break that contrasting stasis and with threatening words he threw his spear forcefully towards the killer of his dear Patroclus. Hector, very skilled and expert, bent his knees, dodged the shaft that passed his head without harming him. For Priam and his followers it was as if they had been liberated after holding their breath and heart in their throats for a very long interminable instant.

It was then the turn of the Priamides: he could have consecrated the victory of Troy with his blow or definitive defeat; he could not fail because he knew very well that Achilles would not be wrong a second time. He firmly threw the shaft and entrusted it with the fate of his people. This hit Achilles' enormous shield and, given its power, it would certainly have broken in two if it had not been of divine manufacture; instead the weapon was rejected without its causing even the slightest scratch on the defensive disk. Hector could not believe his eyes: for a moment he thought he had succeeded (that blow would have overwhelmed any mortal)... He did not want and could not resign himself to the invincibility of that cursed Greek. Then he searched with his eyes for his brother Deiphobus to hand him another spear, but he did not find him and therefore, grasping the sword, he boldly launched himself against the granite Achaean...

Everyone prepared to witness a bloody melee between titans.

But Achilles kept his distance well using the shaft that had been handed to him by a companion and studied his rival's armor carefully seeking an unprotected area of the body; he knew those weapons perfectly, he had worn them hundreds of times in hundreds of battles and he knew that his search would not be easy, given the experience and prowess of the Trojan. However, helped by Pallas Athena and invoking the name of Patroclus, the Greek provoked a sprawling movement of the Priamides. Achilles then glimpsed a very small possible target between the chest and the neck and he planted the shaft there with all his strength, claiming his revenge.

A shiver ran quickly through the surrounding world.

A cry broken by tears rose on the citadel; men and gods motionless witnessed the death of the magnificent Hector, the greatest prince and protector of Troy.

Achilles was then satisfied. Only then did his anger abate. Only then was revenge achieved.

The Greeks exulted sensationally; mindful of the terror they had felt in battle before that Trojan they crowded around the corpse, but Achilles did not allow anyone to rage over the body of the enemy on the ground; stripped of his arms, he tied him by the ankles to the chariot and lashing the horses dragged him ruthlessly for several laps around the walls. Priam, Hecuba and the other Trojans watched helplessly at that hideous massacre.

The divine Apollo, more and more angry with Athena and his father Zeus for allowing his protégé to be killed in this way, quickened the course of the day so that the sun set quickly behind the mountains of Asia.

The Greeks returned joyfully to their camp, aware that from that moment on the war would be easier and shorter.

Achilles, halted the horses, set them free, to take the beautiful body of Hector to his tents, which was now covered with dust mixed with blood, torn by the brushwood and the stones.

THE FUNERAL OF PATROCLUS

The following day hostilities were suspended and awareness of what had occurred became much clearer. The Trojans mourned their prince who had been deprived of a dignified burial and the Greeks were finally able to prepare the funeral of the beloved Patroclus, now worthily avenged.

Achilles had a whole forest cleared to raise the huge stake on which to burn the body of his friend together with sheep, oxen, four beautiful horses, two of his best dogs and twelve young Trojan prisoners; the pyre burned all night until the fire was put out with the wine. Patroclus' ashes, collected in a funeral box, were placed in a large mound on the Troada arena.

After the great ceremony, Achilles, as was the custom, opened the games in memory of the deceased beloved; all the strongest and most valiant Achaean heroes took part and the prizes were chosen from the best spoils of the Pelides war: Diomedes, Menelaus, Antilochus, Meriones and Eumelos, but in the end Diomedes won; Euryalus lost in boxing during the final bout with Epeus; no winner was proclaimed in the fight as Ajax Telamon prevailed in all by force but not against the astute dexterity of Ulysses, who however was unable to defeat his rival definitively; the same king of Ithaca excelled in the foot race preceding Antilochus and Ajax of Oileus, while Ajax Telamon won the spear fencing against Diomedes; in throwing the discus, between Leante, Epeius, Polypoites and the same Ajax Telamon, Polypoites was the best; Meriones imposed himself on Teucer in archery with doves; and so on, until all the rich prizes offered by the king of Myrmidons were exhausted.

THE HUMILIATION OF PRIAM AND THE RETURN OF HECTOR'S BODY

Meanwhile, in Achilles' tent, lay the inanimate body of Hector, visited daily and cleansed with divine oils by Apollo, who continued to protest against the Olympian gods for the unworthy treatment reserved for his protégé. The supreme Zeus, despite the solid opposition of Hera, Athena and Poseidon, ordered Thetis to return Hector's body to the Trojans and immediately sent Hermes to Priam.

Thetis told her son of the divine will.

The old and suffering king of Troy learned the message of the gods, immediately gathered his forces and, mobilized the ambassadors, took a chariot full of gifts outside the city in the direction of the Achaean camp. Hermes guided him to Achilles' tent without anyone stopping him.

As soon as the tired Priam was in front of his son's executioner, he threw himself at his feet like a penitent slave before his master and, taking his hand, began to implore him: "Oh Achilles, your nature is like unto the gods. I pray to you as if I were your father. The great Peleus is now as old as I am but he is certainly less unhappy than I am because he still has his beloved son, invincible and ruthless in battle, and can still hope that one day he will return home. I cannot, no more; I can only implore that my body be mowed down by the same hand that I now humbly put near my lips burned with pain."

"Arise, Priam!" – said Achilles, struck by the noble words of the father – "Arise and sit on my throne. Tonight you will be my guest and tomorrow you can take back your son's corpse. Furthermore, I will grant you eleven days of respite, in which I will restrain the Achaean ranks to allow you and your people to lament and justly bury Prince Hector."

The Trojan king struggled to raise himself off his tired knees, thanked Pelides profusely for what he had been granted but firmly refused to lie with him in that tent and to remain there the whole night.

Thus, some Myrmidons unloaded the Trojan chariot with the rich ransom and there they placed the body of Hector. Thus king Priam, continuously protected and guided by the divine Hermes, was able to return quickly to Troy and deliver the lifeless body of the adored son to the tears of Andromache, Hecuba, Helen and all those who had known the great Hector of Troy in life.

THE AMAZONS OF PENTHESILEA AND THE ETHIOPIANS OF MEMNON

During the eleven days of established truce, while the entire city paid homage to the one who for ten years, every day had been in the front line, had safeguarded the freedom and safety of his people, Agamemnon sent a few ambassadors to Priam to ask for unconditional surrender.

Trojan pride, despite having been mortally wounded, still had a few cards to play ... The ambassadors were returned to the sender.

On the twelfth day, in fact, upon the rekindling of hostilities, two very strong armies came to the aid of Troy: the Amazons, formidable warrior women, led by the beautiful Queen Penthesilea, and the black Ethiopian people, led by the very strong king Memnon, nephew of Priam and son of Eos, goddess of the dawn.

Soon the Greeks, who, with the death of Hector were now certain they would win the long-standing war in a few more days, had to change their mind: the very agile and fast Amazons began to sow terror among the Achaean ranks like, if not more, than the best champions of both sides and every day the black horde of the Ethiopians gained ground, taking the enemy lines a good distance from the walls. Troy could finally catch her breath, she could regain self-confidence, could continue to hope.

Agamemnon and the other Achaean leaders could not believe their own eyes: the most impressive and formidable army of Hellas had been humiliated and overwhelmed by a group of women with a bow on horseback and uncoordinated and disorganized black barbarians. The Achaean Council then decided to beg Achilles' personal help, who had initially refused to fight against those women.

And so, only after a compelling and original duel with Penthesilea, Achilles managed to put an end to that shame for his homeland, wresting the young life and bright beauty from the Amazon queen.

Emulating the deeds of Pelides, old Nestor wanted to do the same with Memnon, who, with the departure of Penthesilea, was the only big thorn in the side of the Achaean hosts.

The Ethiopians, although they were not very many and were not very expert in military strategy, were extremely mobile; shouting they launched into the assault and after striking they managed to escape the counteroffensives quickly and return to hit back on other fronts. The Greeks had never faced a people who fought in that rough but effective way.

During a battle, Nestor managed to present himself face to face before the great Memnon and to aim at him with his spear; nevertheless his tired hand was unable to throw the shaft into the Ethiopian hauberk with the right amount of strength: the weapon barely touched the armor of the black king and fell to the ground. Memnon spun around and petrified the old king of Pylos with his eyes; he would certainly have mowed him down with his arm if his son Antilochus had not come to the rescue, who, having taken up his father's defense, found himself having to directly challenge the offended Ethiopian.

The Achaean leaders well knew that the duel was unequal and that it would not be long before the great Memnon got rid of the young Antilochus, but, out of respect for Nestor, no one intervened to stop the dispute. Achilles also wanted to witness the battle, being strongly connected to Antilochus, especially after the loss of Patroclus.

As was easily foreseen, the sword of the semi-divine Ethiopian king soon had the blood of the young Achaean prince who fell lifeless to the ground.

This could not but provoke the new inevitable revenge of the Pelides, who with Memnon had at least two things in common: divine blood on the part of a mother and deadly weapons of divine manufacture.

Thus began an extraordinary and unforgettable duel between the two. The sun completed its arc in the sky while neither of them managed to have the other succumb despite their enormous inhuman efforts and the ever-growing fury that emanated from both sides.

Only at sunset, with the help of the goddess Athena, Achilles managed to cloud the sight of the son of Eos and at the same time to deliver a terrible sword swing that split the curly head of the latter in two. Memnon collapsed to the ground causing a thunder-like roar to echo across the field; that fatal sound reaffirmed to all the unparalleled strength of the invincible Achilles and advised the Trojans of the end of the last great defender of those still unbroken doors.

THE DEATH OF ACHILLES

The next day Agamemnon brought together all recruits in the Achaean armies to the Council in order to finalize the final assault, the fatal blow that would lead to the fall of Troy and the coveted victorious return to Greece, after ten long and cursed years of bloody war.

Thus, even before the sun appeared on the horizon, the offending black ranks were piled up well beneath the walls, awaiting the order to attack.

The Trojans, now orphaned of the greatest heroes who had sacrificed their lives to defend the myth of that city, were well aware that that day could be the last and, devoid of any pugnacious ambition, more by instinct and habit than anything else, they hurriedly ran to reinforce the doors and protect the walls. Aeneas and Paris, the only ones left to give them a minimum of encouragement, strove in every way to reassure and order the men, but their consideration and their charisma could not even remotely be compared to that of the late Hector.

The attack began.

It soon became clear that the impetus of the Myrmidons and Achilles' determination would create an opening in the Scee gates even before noon. However Zeus had determined that this would be the fatal day for Pelides. The father of all the gods had in fact prevented all creatures of divine nature from taking the side of the

Achaeans the entire day. Thetis too was aware of this and even Achilles in his heart felt that his destiny would soon be fulfilled.

While the fury of the Greeks increased more and more and the extreme resistance of the Trojans became less robust to rush to where the Myrmidons hammered more dangerously, the god Apollo, disobeying Zeus, materialized in the presence of Paris, urging him to face Achilles. Paris trembled like a leaf at the mere idea, refusing to believe that the divine protector of the Trojans and the goddess Aphrodite desired his death after that of many of his other brothers and friends; the sun god then, reassured him, and added that the young man could fight his enemy at a safe distance, staying away from him, since he himself would guide his bow and arrow.

At that point, Paris obeyed: sought Pelides among the crowds, aimed well all along his body and, at the most propitious moment, he shot the dart. The invisible Apollo, as promised, guided its trajectory until the bronze point entered almost entirely into Achilles' heel. The heel was in fact the only vulnerable point in the body of the son of Thetis, who, holding her son by the heel, at an early age, had immersed him in the divine waters of the Styx, which made anyone who were bathed in them invulnerable.

Feeling the blow, Achilles gave a single inhuman cry of pain and fell massively on his knees and then entirely to the ground. A moment later, the greatest of the Achaeans was dead.

Quickly terror coursed across the Achaean camp. Suddenly the threat had ended and the injured hoards moved towards the Scee gates.

Agamemnon and Menelaus, then Ulysses, Ajax and Diomedes rushed to the fatal point; still incredulous they recovered the body of the great Achilles, before he ended up with his weapons in the hands of the Trojans, and carried him on a chariot, ordering the retreat. Thetis, the Nereids and the Muses also rushed to the Achaean tents.

They cried for 17 days and 17 nights.

THE MADNESS OF AJAX

After the most memorable hero of that expedition was
given a dignified burial, in the presence of which even the great
Agamemnon went into the shadows, an animated dispute arose in
the Achaean camp about who among the Greek leaders was the
most worthy to possess the weapons of the Pelides.

After endless harangue and praise of deeds and
achievements made by both heroes, the favors of the most
influential of princes were divided equally between the supporters
of Ajax Telamon of Salamis and those of Ulysses of Ithaca.

Given the perfect equality between the two final candidates,
Agamemnon decided to involve the troops in the choice, but even
these were divided almost equally as well as their leaders. Finally
the servants, the workers, the craftspeople and the prisoners were
finally called to judge... Even the gods were now weary of that
dispute; then Athena, goddess of war but also of knowledge and
wisdom, through the mouth of an old Trojan prisoner ruled:
"Without the sword and might of Ajax, but not without the
hindsight of Ulysses can the citadel of Troy be conquered".

On hearing these words the crowd fell silent and the silence
assumed the appearance of a sublime divine assertion.

"The decision has been made!" – exclaimed the king of
kings and handed the weapons of Achilles to Ulysses. The meeting
broke up and everyone returned, albeit whispering about their own
occupations.

The defeated Ajax, on the other hand, remained there alone, dumb, astonished, motionless, almost petrified, and then suddenly exploded in a violent and furious shout of anger; he became pale and then his face bruised and, passing everything in his path, he ran out of the tents; he put a threatening hand on his sword and began to angrily shout out all the names of the Achaean leaders.

These, fearing the Telamon, were astonished, but then they saw him with blood shot eyes go towards the fenced flocks and there he chased and massacred the largest beasts. All watched helplessly, astonished at that senseless slaughter, and only then did they understand what absurd madness had struck the great Ajax. And only when the last ram, which he called Ulysses, was massacred and crushed, did the madness, infused by Athena, leave the mind of poor Ajax.

At last he came to his senses, the hero learned and saw with his own eyes what he had done and the shameful spectacle he had displayed to his companions and his soldiers, covering the noble and proud house of Telamon with ridicule and infamy. While everyone still stared at him in amazement, Ajax now composed and determined, went to the sea, cleansed his body and arms of the blood of the animals, returned, took up the sword given to him by Hector and headed back to the beach; there, he invoked Zeus, Hermes and the Erinyes, he planted the hilt of the sword in the sand and, after a last glance at the walls of Troy, let his mighty body fall on the silver point that pierced him from one side to the other. Thus died the great Ajax.

THE THREE CONDITIONS

Days passed after that unfortunate affair without the Achaeans being able to find a solution to end the cursed war that Agamemnon had strongly desired above all else.

The Trojans began to breathe again, attempting alliances with neighboring peoples.

One night, Ulysses, who was on patrol around the Scee gates in search of something that would cause his sly mind to give birth to one of his tricks, was intrigued by some strange movements, saw Elenus, son of Priam and priest of Apollo, who came out of the great gates in the direction of the enemy camp. The Ithacan hidden following a few steps after, then he jumped up from behind him and ordered him to stop. The young prince obeyed; certain that Ulysses would never dare to take his life since the god Apollo protected it, who had already been responsible for many misfortunes among the Greeks. In fact, Ulysses, who had previously blamed Agamemnon's mistake against Chryses, would never have moved a finger against that boy, but still tried to exploit that capture to his favor; he led Helenus to his tents and politely asked him to question the gods about the mystery of the inviolability of Troy.

The oracle prince, by his divine vow, could not refuse, if worthily questioned, to manifest what the god would suggest; therefore he agreed to serve the Greek hero as long as he gave Apollo a solemn offering of extraordinary fauna. Agamemnon was immediately informed and the sacrifice was made; an odorous smoke rose from the massacre and pervaded the whole field.

The god was satisfied and ordered Helenus to respond as follows: "All efforts and machinations devised by the Achaeans will be in vain for another ten and a hundred years, until three golden conditions are met: a son of Zeus must rain arrows on Troy; another man of divine descent must fight against Troy using divine weapons; goddess friend must be removed and abducted from Troy". Such was Apollo's cryptic response through Helenus' mouth and everyone was stunned and confused.

By order of Ulysses, the young Trojan prince was left free to return to his city, although some of the Greek leaders would have liked to keep him to question him more deeply about that senseless decree, incomprehensible even to the wisest and most experienced of priests.

What did those three conditions mean?

While everyone was wondering and trying to decipher the divine message, the usual Ulysses had a flash of clairvoyance and, applauded by the bystanders, managed to reveal the first two conundrums: the son of Zeus mentioned in the first condition would have been the great Heracles who at point of death had delivered his infallible arrows to Philoctetes, who had been abandoned by his companions on the island of Lemnos along with his providential darts; the second condition instead recalled the late Achilles, son of Peleus and the divine Thetis, whose weapons had been forged by the god Hephaestus himself. Ulysses, in fact, was aware of a secret that Achilles had never revealed to anyone, namely that, during his stay in Skyros, Pelides had secretly joined with Deidamia, the lovely daughter of King Lycomedes, and a son had been born from their union, Neoptolemus; therefore, by bringing the latter to war and equipping him with the paternal weapons, the second condition would also be satisfied.

- 87 -

PHILOCTHETES, NEOPTOLEMUS AND THE DEATH OF PARIS

In that way, a few days later, Agamemnon let Ulysses set

sail with the fastest ship in the fleet to quickly recover and bring back Philoctetes and Neoptolemus.

Everyone knew that it was not at all easy to find and persuade the two nobles to rush to Troy (especially Philoctetes who had certainly not so quickly forgotten how he had been abandoned), but Ulysses was the only one able to complete that mission and in fact in the end he succeeded: Philoctetes was healed of the excruciating wound and Neoptolemus was persuaded to put on his father's sacred weapons to seek revenge among the Trojans.

As soon as the three met at the Achaean war machine, the consequences for Priam and his followers were catastrophic: no Trojan could go outside the walls without exposing themselves to the risk of being hit from a very great distance by the deadly arrows of Philoctetes or of being terrified and mowed down by the unparalleled weapons of the young Neoptolemus.

And it was precisely because of a herculean dart that even Paris lost his life, the one who had triggered the pretentious fuse of that war, the one who had killed the great Achilles, the one who was loved and hated by the Trojans had represented the last defense of the house of Priam: Philoctetes methodically aimed at Paris, Athena strongly inhibited the protective action of Aphrodite, a divine arrow, let fly in the memory of Heracles and Achilles, shivered in the air until it struck the beautiful neck of the Trojan prince killing him; thus died Paris, the most beautiful of men.

For days the beautiful Helen and the maternal Hecuba cried desperately over the body of their beloved companion and son. Old Priam and Troy mourned all the horrendous loss of yet another prince of Ilium. The divine Aphrodite mourned the death of Love won by the fatal design of Reason, which by now, by the will of Zeus, had decreed the fall of Troy.

THE ABDUCTION OF THE PALLADIUM

First, however, the enigma of the third condition of Helenus had to be solved. The oracle Calchas provided this, finally managing to answer Agamemnon's insistent and threatening questions.

The *goddess friend*, mentioned in the prophecy, was certainly not an allied deity of the Trojans, but it must have been Pallas Athena, who had been a friend to the Achaeans since the beginning of the war.

The Palladium was, in fact, kept in Troy, an ancient wooden statuette of Athena that the gods had given to the ancient king Ilus, predicting that the city he founded would be impregnable as long as that simulacrum remained inside the walls. This was therefore the object that had to be stolen; such was the mission to be carried out to put an end to that interminable war.

Ulysses and Diomedes offered themselves as volunteers for the expedition, who, in a dark night, after days that the Trojans no longer went out in battle, managed to sneak secretively among merchants and, once inside the city, they skillfully carried out the abduction of the Palladium.

Only the following day, when the Trojans went to the temple, did they notice the disappearance of the statuette and many, believing this to be divine work, a sign of Providence that definitively sentenced the imminent end of any residual resistance, gave themselves to death.

THE HORSE AND SINON

Days of unusual and unlikely quiet followed.

The Trojans, who for some time remained strictly confined within the walls, guilty of having allowed the Palladium to be stolen, filled the temples with gifts and sacrifices in an extreme attempt to appease the wrath of Athena.

The Greeks, for their part, while being able to strike the now very weak enemy and to shortly end the game, also avoided leaving the camp, except to gather huge supplies of wood in the surrounding forests. Even the Achaean soldiers and officers were unable to understand what was taking place. Why not take advantage of that long-awaited moment and then remain idle being woodcutters?

The best informed in the camp recounted that, following one of the usual war forums, a harangue by Ulysses of Ithaca had managed to convince Agamemnon and the other leaders to break the lines of the ranks already ordered to attack; then Ulysses himself was seen to come out of his tent and order Epeius to build a huge equine-shaped wooden sculpture. From that moment on, weapons were abandoned to hold saws, hammers and planers. The men worked hard but did not understand what the senseless effort and the useless waste of time could accomplish.

The apparent situation of extraordinary stasis continued for days, until one clear morning a Trojan lookout, not believing his own eyes, saw a long line of fire and smoke in the direction of the Greek camp: there were no more external defenses, the camp was a disaster, as if hurriedly abandoned during the previous night, the ships had sailed away taking away that huge contingent of men and armaments that for ten years had softened and tormented that beautiful and flourishing land reducing it to desolation and misery.

Antenor and Aeneas and subsequently Deiphobus and Priam were informed immediately; the entire population gathered on the walls to confirm the incredible news. Nobody dared believe the war was truly over.

After a few hours, legitimately suspicious and timidly curious, a handful of men cautiously went out to check what could be seen from afar. All was confirmed and soon the theories of ambush and hidden pitfalls were forestalled. Then came the other Trojan leaders and soldiers and finally Priam, the elderly, women and children. The enemy, with the terror that accompanied it, was incredibly and inexplicably gone.

Everything had been destroyed. But on the seashore, where the black ships had been, now stood, motionless among the pines and oleanders, a mammoth wooden structure, enormous, taller than the centuries-old pine trees and the walls of Troy themselves. It was shaped like a giant horse, including mane and tail.

Priam and his men approached it cautiously and silently. They looked around it in amazement, then they touched it and someone began to speculate about what it could be or could mean.

A supernatural being? A monster? A war machine designed to storm the walls? What else?

And why did it have that shape? And why had the Greeks never deployed it in war? And why didn't they set it on fire like all the rest of the things around there? Each had at least three questions like these and, failing to give as many coherent and admissible answers, they began to invoke the divinatory help of fortune-tellers, assuming that such a creation could be sacred to some god.

As people unconsciously began to retreat, Laocoon, priest of Poseidon, stepped forward, who, severely, blaming his fellow citizens saying: – "Crazy, foolish! Do not be taken in by the unconscious joy of this unexpected incidence. You're vision and reason have been distorted! Deception is always around the corner. Have you already forgotten the thousand tricks of the Greeks? Their boundless pride, merciless ambition and determination to conduct the war for years? Don't think you won the war that easily! This construction is by no means sacred. It is just a wooden monster and you have to destroy it!" – Then the priest threw a rod against the horse's belly, silencing the bystanders.

In the meantime, a couple of men who had been sent on patrol returned with a poor rag dirty with blood and mud; they dragged it into the shouting crowd and threw it at Priam's feet to decide what to do with it. King Priam learned that the man had voluntarily surrendered himself to his soldiers in the reed beds of the Scamanda and began to interrogate him.

He looked dreadful, seemed exhausted and hungry. He was a Greek, and his name was Sinon. While, with a few worn teeth, he tore at some pieces of meat the Trojans offered him, he began to tell his sad story: he had been following Palamedes for years, the Greek hero that was hated by Ulysses for having forced him to undertake the expedition against Troy, and, from the moment his leader had been the victim of the king of Ithaca's revenge, he had refused to fight alongside the latter, openly accused of inhuman shrewdness and cruelty that was ill-concealed behind a cold and calculating wisdom. Thus, on the occasion of the last human sacrifice to be made to appease the wrath of the gods before returning safely to Greece, the Achaean Leaders, under the intrigues of the usual Ulysses, had decided to immolate the poor Sinon on the burning pyre. Except that, at the time of throwing the fatal dagger, a flash in the sky blinded the participants of the ritual for minutes and the designated victim finding his wrists and ankles free, managed to escape and hide in the surrounding woods, hunted for days by his own compatriots, before they finally set sail. In fact, he did not represent only a simple sacrificial victim like many others, just as the simulated rite had not been celebrated according to custom. It had happened – Sinon went on to say – that strange deaths occurred in the Greek camp following the abduction of the Palladium from the sacred temple of Troy. At first Ulysses and Diomedes, the architects of the theft were accused of that great misfortune and then even Agamemnon, who had ordered that sacrilegious mission to be carried out. In the end it was decided, as was usual in such cases, to interrogate the fortune teller Calchas, who ruled that the wrath of Athena would only be appeased if the defiled Palladium was delivered to Poseidon in the depths of the sea, if in its place a new simulacrum consecrated to the goddess was built and left in that place and if the life of a man of worthy origins was sacrificed in his honor. And so Ulysses, giving free rein to his ingenuity and his good oratory art, took the occasion to enrich the architect Epeius, to whom he still owed several talents, and at the same time to eliminate another of his enemies: so Epeius was commissioned to build an enormous wooden simulacrum with the appearance of a horse and Sinon was sentenced to death.

At that point in the story the eyes of the filthy prisoner began to tear, his hands pushed back the food and his mouth stopped moving, and speaking and chewing.

Priam then believed in the good faith of the poor man in front of him and ordered that he be helped to get up and be cleaned and dressed in a manner appropriate to his rank. Before dismissing him, however, he had a final question for him: he still could not understand why anyone wanted that horse and why it had been conceived in such a mammoth size, so much as to be frightening. Sinon promptly replied that even in this case it was a subtle trick of the hated Ulysses: the new simulacrum, a replacement for the Palladium, should have been larger than the walls of Troy, so that, not being able to bring it with him to Greece, not even the Trojans would have been able to return it to their temple and, therefore, Troy could no longer go back to being impregnable. King Priam said he was satisfied with this logical response; he dismissed the Achaean, giving him freedom and offering him the hospitality of his people.

The best sages and technicians gathered in parliament to discuss what to do with that simulacrum, in the light of the revelations of Sinon the Greek.

Among the sages and priests the opinion prevailed not to destroy but to preserve that consecrated symbol which, in place of the Palladium, would protect the city in future centuries. The technicians, however, could not fail to note that Ulysses' acute mind had hit the mark again and could not fail to demonstrate to their king that it was impossible to let the titanic wooden construction enter the city through the doors without dividing it or dissecting it into several pieces. But the wise men and the priests strongly opposed this hypothesis, reaffirming the sacredness of the object in its entirety.

Only Laocoon firmly affirmed his opposition to worship that monstrous monument of which nothing was known with certainty except for the suspicious story of a foreigner. But while the learned priest of Apollo ended his lively intervention, a strange foam generated in the sea that quickly approached the shore; two long mighty sea snakes emerged from the frothy wave which, in a few moments, arrived on the beach and wrapped around Laocoon and his two sons, immobilizing them with several coils and finally biting them on the neck and on the head. Immediately and horribly the bodies of the three collapsed lifelessly and the snakes proceeded in the direction of the temple of Athena, where someone saw them gather and enter the shield of the statue of the goddess. All the bystanders were terrified and unable to fully interpret what had happened.

After a fairly long meditation, despite the protests and the unfortunate predictions of Princess Cassandra, Priam ordered part of the walls above the doors to be demolished, so that the horse could be led whole into the city and placed near the temple of Pallas Athena.

At this resolution the crowd cheered; some rushed to organize the celebrations for the night, others hurried to build the mobile supports to carry the abnormal equine construction, others strove on the white stone to breach the walls. They worked hard until the evening but the effort did not seem to scratch in the least the physicists and the minds of the Trojans who, finally, exulted and celebrated the finish of the endless war.

When the horse was taken to its destination, everyone began to feast around a huge massacre that Priam had requested to thank the gods. The young people went wild in dances and games and the elders finally released their hearts from any anxiety and pain accumulated in ten years of nightmares. Late at night everyone was satiated with food, wine, peace and joy and abandoned their limbs to sleep. Troy saved was shrouded in a warm silence.

THE FALL OF TROY

But not everyone was asleep, not Sinon the Greek; he
had managed to deceive even Morpheus. Ending his masterful
simulation, he awoke, looked around him, ran near the horse and
let out a strange hiss.

A small door slowly opened in the belly of the horse, from
which a strong rope dangled. Gradually a man dropped from the
rope: it was the irreproachable Ulysses, and behind him Menelaus
and then Diomedes and Sthenelus and Neoptolemus and five more,
another ten and twenty daring Achaean warriors. Some ran
cautiously to the city gates, others, with Sinon, climbed the walls
with burning torches in their hands and made a great fire there: it
was the signal.

In short, the entire Achaean fleet in full command of
Agamemnon invaded the sea again, not even a thousand feet from
the beach. It was ready to attack after hiding behind the island of
Tenedos during the day.

While the Trojans slept unsuspectingly in their own homes,
thousands of Greeks breached the wide open doors, silent but
ruinous as a plague, into the fortress and quickly seized the walls
and nerve points of the city.

Quickly, a large part of the Greek army was inside Troy: the
silence suddenly turned to shouting, cursing and screaming. After
the squares, houses, temples and palaces were invaded and burned.
The city awoke and found itself in a flash of hell, of crashes, flames

and tumult: men were barbarously slaughtered while still asleep and terrified women were raped in their nuptial beds.

Menelaus, with Sinon and his family, ran towards the house of the young prince Deiphobus, brother-in-law and spouse of Helen after the death of Paris. When he arrived, he ordered the door to be knocked down and impetuously entered it, while the landlord, naked, surprised in his sleep, fought against him. Menelaus, bloodthirsty, massacred him with blows, climbed over the corpse and proceeded determined in the direction of the innermost rooms for the women, in his furious search for Helen, determined to dip his blooded sword into the bosom of the most loved, most cursed, most fated of woman. But as soon as he saw her, beautiful, shining, pale, noble, incredibly serene, dressed only in a peplum with gold embroidery on which her blonde hair fell loose, he stopped suddenly, as if surprised by a divine vision.

Helen sinuously came towards him offering him a cup of the sweetest wine, just as she had done on other occasions in Sparta on the return of her husband from hunting trips. Menelaus remained motionless for a few moments before that splendor of beauty, sweetness and regal serenity, then, assailed by a whirlwind of memories and passion, fascinated he drank the nectar the bewitching woman offered him; he held Helen in his arms, bringing her to his chest and fixing his eyes and said to her: "Come. For you, for you alone, all this cursed war has been fought." And while his men raped and slaughtered handmaids and servants, he dragged her through the city to his ship.

Menelaus' war could thus be considered ended, but certainly not that of Agamemnon, Ajax of Oileus, Neoptolemus and the other Achaean leaders who had waited for that moment for years and who now would not have given up anything in the world to give free reign to heinous revenge, looting, raiding, thirst for blood and lust for power.

Neoptolemus was the first to enter the palace of Priam, massacring dozens of loyal Trojan defenders, before ruthlessly sinking the blade of Achilles into the body of Priam and his son Polite. Agamemnon and his men soon stole the royal treasure. Princess Polissena, torn from the arms of her mother Hecuba, was enslaved, as was Andromache. Neoptolemus entrusted the two young women to one of his men to be led to his ship, while he, revenge still not sated, threw the little Astyanax son of Hector, Achilles' great rival, down from a tower.

And it was exactly Hector, while his Troy was now lost, while everything was destroyed, while the flames burned the living and the dead, appeared in a dream to Aeneas, his brother-in-law and last hero of the Trojan resistance; he urged him to awaken and to run to the extreme defense of his king, his family and the Penates, the simulacra of the Trojan gods who had always protected his people.

But it was too late... the massive massacre was now complete.

Aeneas, out on the street, blinded by fury and remorse at not having been able to prevent the massacre, was ready to fight for the last time and find death between the iron and the fire of his beloved homeland. But at that instant, in that hell, his mother Aphrodite materialized before him. In a few words the goddess eased the mind of her beloved son, causing him to regain his lucidity and composure and to desist from any heroic intent of extreme desperate defense, but to save himself with his family, taking away with him the sacred Penates, to find a new worthy seat beyond the sea, in another land, where a great nation, new ruler and light of the world over the centuries, would be founded by his offspring on the ashes of Troy.

So, Aeneas, having recovered the idol of the homeland, ran home, where fortunately the invaders' bloodthirsty fury had not yet raged; he took his son Iulus Ascanius by the hand, hoisted his father Anchises on his shoulders and ordered his wife Creusa to follow him. Together with a few other Trojans, hidden and protected by Aphrodite, the four managed to leave their homes unharmed and to secure themselves in the temple of Demeter on a nearby mountain. From there, terrified, they watched the flames, the smoke and the funereal blanket that enveloped the city, Troy, Ilium, the splendid phoenix now dead would rise in the west more beautiful, more powerful and eternal.

APPENDIX A - "THE GREEK GODS"

The images and photos in this appendix are taken from "Mythica Encyclopedia - www.pantheon.org"

Zeus

Hera

Apollo

Artemis

Hermes

Athena

Dionysus

Ares

Aesculapius

Hecate

APPENDIX B - "GENEALOGIES"

The images and photos in this appendix are taken from "Encyclopedia Mythica
–www.pantheon.org"

Genealogy of the main gods of Greek mythology

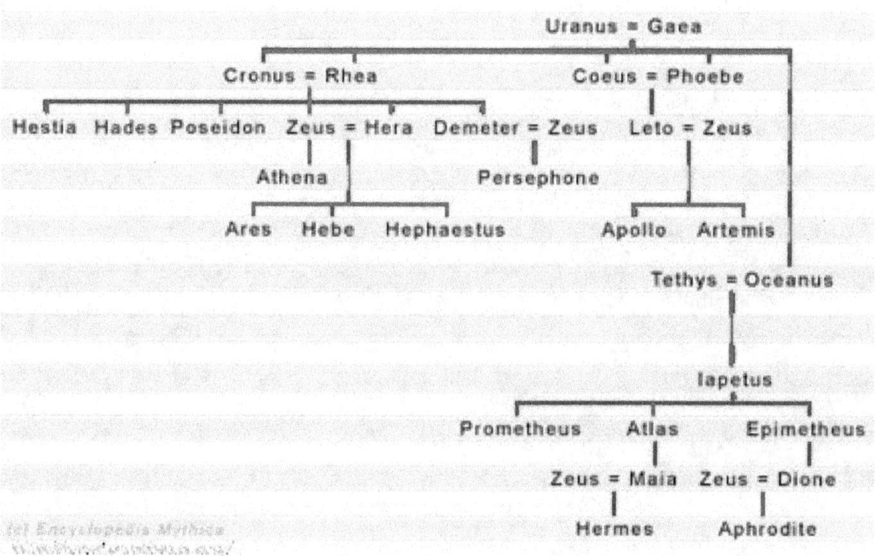

Consorts and relative mortal offspring of Zeus

Mother	Offspring
Alcmene	Heracles
Antiope	Amphion, Zethus
Callisto	Arcas
Danae	Perseus
Aegina	Aeacus
Electra	Dardanus, Harmonia, Iasius
Europa	Minos, Rhadamanthys, Sarpedon
Io	Epaphus
Laodamia	Sarpedon
Leda	Polydeuces (Pollux), Helen
Niobe	Argos, Pelasgus
nymph	Tantalus
Semele	Dionysus
Taygete	Lacadaemon

The royal house of Troy

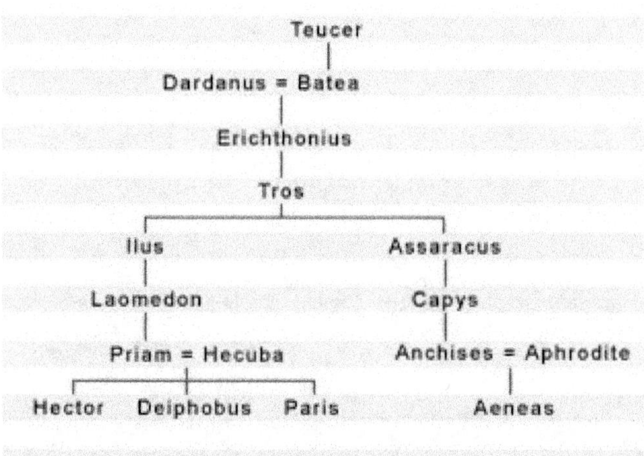

Genealogy of Helen

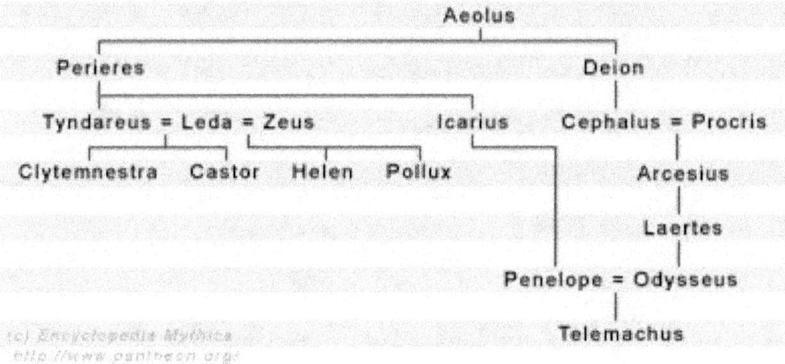

Achilles genealogy

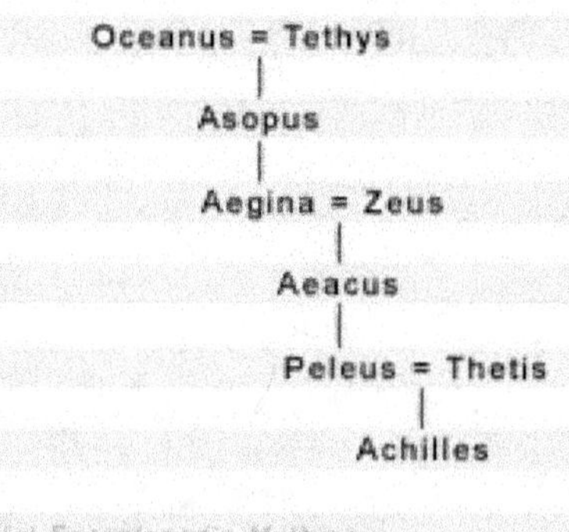

Descendants of Prometheus

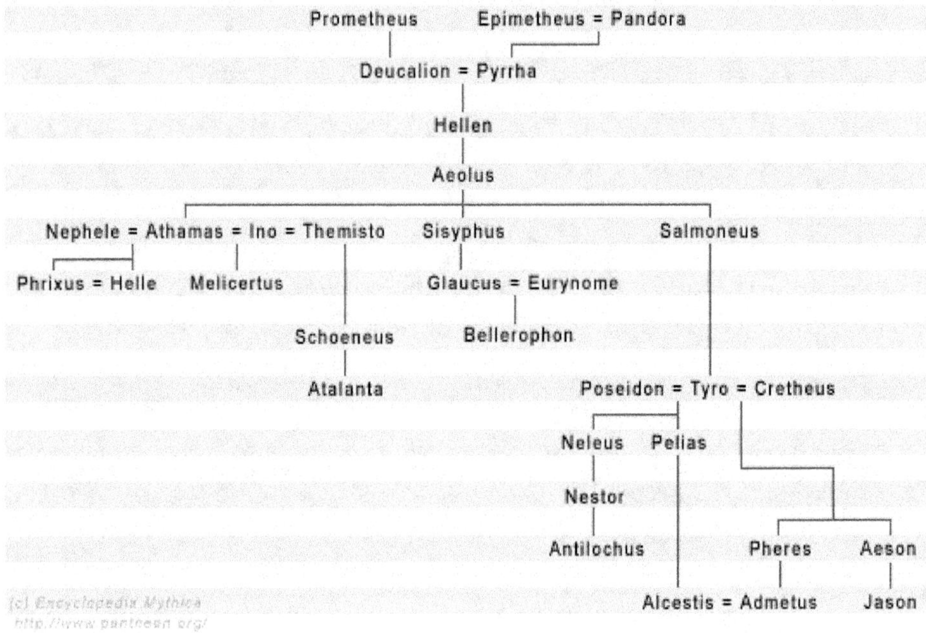

APPENDIX C – "GREECE AND TROY"

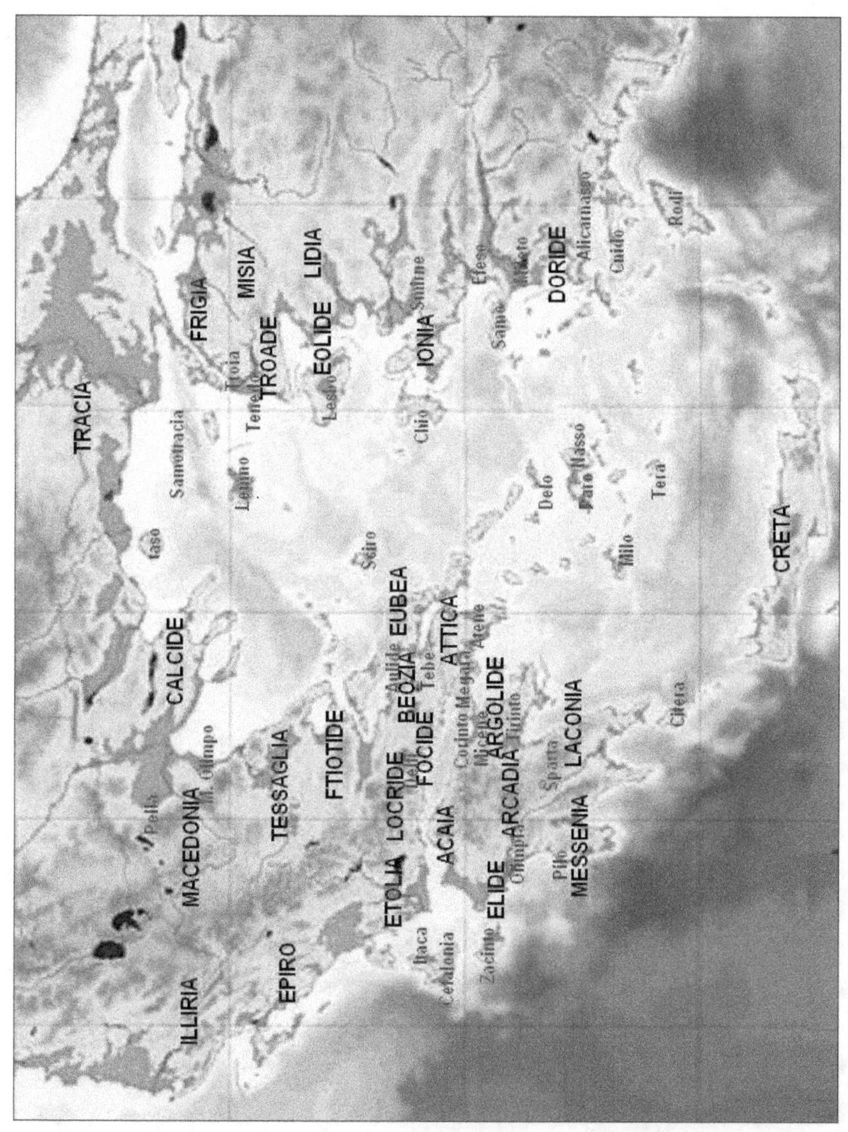

THE AUTHOR

Engineer, professor, trainer and popularizer of science, Dionigi Cristian Lentini was born in Mottola, in Apulian Lower Murgia, in 1980. Author of ''Pantheon Magnorum'', ''Fictional History of the Trojan War'', ''Praising - Praise of the Engineer'', '' Like a butterfly'', "9 miliardi di oscillazioni di Cesio", etc. You can find his complete biography on the website: www.cristianlentini.

Dionigi Cristian Lentini, engineer, professor, scientific popularizer and writer, in 1998 came second in the "Premio Nazionale Ori di Taranto".
Passionate about mythology and ancient history, he is the author of several historical essays and chronologies, which have been published from 2000 to today.

In 2016 he published "Tecnologie wired e wireless: protocolli di sicurezza delle reti di comunicazione" (Wired and wireless technologies: communication network security protocols), "Cryptography: la crittografia alla base delle tecnologie modern" (Cryptography: cryptography at the basis of modern technologies", "Hacking Technology – Tecnologie e Hackers (Hacking Technology – Technology and Hackers) and the poetry collection "Come una farfalla" (Like a butterfly).

In 2018 it was the turn of "9 miliardi di oscillazioni di Cesio" (9 billion oscillations of Cesio) and the essay "PraisING – Elogio dell'ingegnere" (PraisENG - In praise of the engineer).
The latest novel, bestselling among the historical thrillers of late 2019, is L'uomo che sedusse la Gioconda (The Man Who Seduced the Gioconda).

Since 2017 he has been full professor of Technology at the Ministry of Education, of the University and of Research and President of the ICT Commission of the Order of Engineers of Taranto.

BIBLIOGRAPHY

- Birardi F. 1938. *Ilio's novel*, Felice Le Monnier, Florence.
- Crocitto, Garozzo, Tucci. 1992. *EPICA*, Lucarini School.
- Graves R. *THE GREEK MYTHS*, Historical Library – *Il Giornale.*
- Grant, M., Hazel J. 1986. *DICTIONARY OF CLASSICAL MYTHOLOGY*, SugarCo Edizioni.
- Homer. 1903. *ILIADE* (translated by V. Monti), Salesian Library.
- Mythica Encyclopedia: www.pantheon.org
- Wikipedia: www.wikipedia.it

The cover image is taken from the work "The Loves of Paris and Helen" by Jacques-Louis David, 1788

www.ingramcontent.com/pod-product-compliance
Lightning Source LLC
LaVergne TN
LVHW010633200726
843507LV00011B/1696